All the rooms were wrecked and bare and contained nothing but ammunition, the guards' bare pallets, and piles of rotting garbage. God, but these men are pigs, thought Cowboy, as he slaughtered one.

Right through the heart. The second man turned with his rifle. And kept turning. Because his head exploded, spraying Cowboy with blood and brains.

The last room had just one man. Cowboy pushed open the door and took aim at the head of the man who was firing out the window. He wasn't quiet enough. The man heard him. He turned. Cowboy was already squeezing the trigger.

"Cowboy," the target said. "You bastard . . ."

Cowboy fired.

DEADLY
REUNION

BOOKS BY MICHAEL MCDOWELL AND JOHN PRESTON

THE BLACK BERETS

Deadly Reunion
Cold Vengeance
The Black Palm
Contract: White Lady
Louisiana Firestorm
The Death Machine Contract
The Red Man Contract
D.C. Death March
The Night of the Jaguar
Contract: Terror Summit
The Samurai Contract
The Akbar Contract
Blue Water Contract

DEADLY REUNION

MICHAEL MCDOWELL AND JOHN PRESTON

BLACK STONE

PUBLISHING

ISBN 979-8-200-88180-2
Fiction / War & Military

Version 1

Blackstone Publishing
31 Mistletoe Rd.
Ashland, OR 97520

www.BlackstonePublishing.com

For Marvin Preston, USMC

Long have they pass'd, faces and trenches and fields,
Where through the carnage I moved with a callous composure, or away from the fallen,
Onward I sped at the time—but now of their forms at night, I dream, I dream, I dream.
                                    —Walt Whitman,
                                        "Old War-Dreams"

1

Billy Leaps Beeker hadn't wanted to do anything that Sunday afternoon but maybe hunt some woodchuck. With his HK770, freshly cleaned and carefully loaded, he was walking through the forests no more than a mile from his home. He knew this forest. He walked here often. It was quiet, though Billy Leaps was quieter. Here, in this Louisiana forest of oak and loblolly pine, he could count on being alone. That was important. He liked being alone. Get off a few woodchuck, he thought, and it would be a nice day.

It was winter, but winter isn't a harsh season in Louisiana, not even in the northwestern corner of the state. The hickories and the persimmons had lost their leaves, but the oaks still clung to theirs, and would cling to them till the spring, when new growth pushed the old dead leaves off their branches. Billy Leaps imagined he was a Cherokee warrior, one of his ancestors, hunting in the forest for game for his family. He tested himself to see how quietly he could make his way through these silent, needle-carpeted woods. At one time that effort would have counted as training. His life would have depended on his abilities. Now it was just a game.

Yet Beeker's dress suggested that he was taking the game seriously. He wore his old Marine-issue hat, a cap made of camouflage tiger stripe material. Over his olive drab thermal shirt he wore his old tiger stripe shirt, worn thin in the fifteen years since it had been part of his uniform. His pants were denim jeans. His boots were military-issue black leather lace-ups. Not the jungle boots he had been accustomed to wearing with his uniform, but still, from their spit polish, it was apparent there was still a lot of the Marine left in Billy Leaps. A lot of Marine.

He was a big man. Six one and over two hundred pounds of hard muscle. Not an inch of it had gone to fat. He was thirty-six, but Marine training was still evident in every ounce of his flesh. His deeply tanned skin was taut over muscle and sinew. His jet-black hair, hidden under his cap, had been cut in the high inside fashion of a jarhead since he had enlisted in the Marines eighteen years before. His lips were thin, a straight hard line across the lower part of his face. His jaw was deep and square, his cheekbones high and hard, giving a wide expanse of slightly sunken cheek. In certain light his head looked like a skull, hastily recovered with a thin layer of flesh. He was an Indian, and his Cherokee blood wasn't disguised even by the light blue eyes that seemed almost incandescent against the toughened skin of his face.

The lower part of his left ear had been blown off. It didn't seem as much a disfigurement as an indication of the ferocity that lay behind the impenetrable, stoic exterior of Billy Leaps's face. A signpost of danger. He wasn't self-conscious about the wound. On those rare occasions he caught a glimpse of himself in the mirror, the mangled ear seemed right. Something like that had happened on the inside of him, too.

He walked silently, and he listened. Listened for game. It was the easiest thing in the world to judge an animal's size and weight by the sound it made moving through the forest. It was almost as easy to judge the degree of its timidity. Now that the bear, the puma, and the lynx had disappeared from these Louisiana forests, all the animals were timid. Frightened.

Then Billy Leaps heard something, and the sound had nothing at all to do with timidity and fear. Nothing at all It was the unmistakable sound that flesh made when it hit flesh. And hit flesh hard.

In Billy Leaps's forest it was an intrusive sound, like a cash register ringing in a church sanctuary.

He heard laughter too.

Instinct shot a small charge of adrenaline through him. His mouth twitched, and the game turned into something else. He crouched and ran through the forest, augmenting the Cherokee's natural stealth with his own training. Before, when he had only been hunting woodchuck, his movement had not been quiet, not really. Nothing had been at stake. Just woodchucks. His alertness had been mechanical, stiff. There was nothing stiff or mechanical about the way he was moving now. His heart pumped adrenaline through every vein, but Billy Leaps's training was even capable of bringing an adrenaline high under control. He was one undivided mass of alertness and readiness.

He came to a small clearing. Lightning had struck several months back and burned out a few dozen trees. The forest hadn't yet retaken the scorched ground.

Billy Leaps smiled grimly, a smile just for himself. He had known it; he had known it in his gut when he first heard the noises and the laughter. He had found prey worth going after. Something bigger than woodchuck. A man knew, that was all. When you had been trained the way Billy Leaps was trained, you knew. The smile on his face, even though it was private, didn't last long. What he saw in the clearing made him too angry to maintain it. That brief smile faded. His hands clutched the rifle, his finger went to the safety and released it.

The anger was like a drug in his veins. It made his body hot, from the pit of his belly to the pores of his skin.

On the far side of the clearing was a boy, no more than sixteen. He stood with his back to a tree, his arms twisted around the thick trunk, his hands tied behind. Another rope was lashed tightly about his calves. A third rope went around his neck. Whenever the boy turned his head, the coarse fibers of the rope cut across the flesh of his neck. Even from this distance Billy Leaps could see the horizontal wound forming there.

Billy Leaps could also see that the boy was Indian.

He knew that as surely as he knew that the two men standing in front of the boy were his prey. The prey that was infinitely better than woodchuck.

His prey was human.

Two men. Whites. One, near Billy Leaps's own age, was slothfully fat with years of beer bloating his belly. The flesh of his bare arms quivered and swung with near-atrophy. He disgusted Billy Leaps.

The other was younger, in his early twenties. He was skinny but had the same blond hair as the older, fat man. His mouth, open in a grotesque smile, was made positively hideous by the rotted teeth that showed there. He was enjoying the pain of the Indian boy.

Just the sight of the two men on the street would have made Billy Leaps nauseous. But what they were doing to the boy stifled the nausea and brought his anger to the fore. A lifetime of anger. The anger of generations of Cherokee before him.

The fat white man was screaming at the boy.

"Thought I tol' you never to come back here, you goddamn red-skinned bastard." He had a fringe of pale yellow hair around the sunburnt crown of his bald head. He wore the clothes of a dirt farmer: denim overalls and a denim workshirt. They were not scrupulously clean, but they had given long service struggling with his obese gut.

This older man was one of those who hang around in derelict bars, taking up with stupid kids who didn't see the waste that was his life. He had to find young, inexperienced men—boys, really—who'd respond to his boasts and his ridiculous inauthentic macho. You could see it in the way he looked to the skinny man for approval every time he threw another punch. What thirty-six-year-old needs that kind of approval from a red-neck punk as ignorant as himself, and only half as old?

His young friend, however, gave his approval with a single nod of his head. The dirt farmer grinned proudly and pulled himself up straighter.

Then he brought back his fist and rammed it into the boy's stomach. The boy's mouth opened in a frantic twist of pain, but the cry was silent. Because there was no cry, Billy Leaps could hear the sharp noise that was the unmistakable sound of a rib cracking. He hadn't heard it in a while, not for years, but he knew a cracking rib like he knew the sound of his own voice. The boy quickly clenched his jaw and glared back at the blond farmer. Unwilling tears ran from his eyes and poured down his cheeks until they merged with two rivulets of bloody mucus seeping from his already broken nose.

Billy Leaps looked at the boy and saw courage like none he had witnessed in years. The boy wouldn't break. The boy glared at his attackers. His breath emerged noisy and labored from his mouth, and he struggled to bring it under control. Billy Leaps, invisible on the far side of the clearing, nodded approval.

The skinny attacker wasn't quite so ridiculous. But a great deal meaner. He carried a rifle, just a twenty-two for small game.

He casually lifted the sharp and vicious barrel and poked it into the boy's wounded stomach, knowing that the sudden pressure on the broken rib would translate into torture.

The boy's mouth opened wide as the metal prodded at the injury beneath his skin. His breath was choked off for a few moments. Still no sound came. He glared at the men through his tears. He refused to submit.

Another time the fat man hit the boy, now on his face. The boy's head jerked widely aside. An obscene wave of tears and blood and mucus flew through the air and slapped onto the needle-strewn ground of the Louisiana forest.

The fat man turned to his companion. "Think he's had enough fun, Joe? Or are we gonna teach this stealing bastard a real lesson?"

Joe, the meaner one, said nothing. He only smiled. He hadn't moved the barrel of the rifle from the boy's stomach, but he hadn't applied pressure either. Now he jerked it upward. The boy's head snapped back with a report against the rough bark of the tree to which he was secured. His breath came noisily through his clenched teeth. He tried to blink away his tears, but they came too fast.

"Who's gonna know if there's one less useless redskin in this part of the country? Maybe the welfare department." He laughed. "But nobody else. Nobody else is gonna care. Hell," Joe went on, the laughter gone, "we tol' him. We warned him. Who's gonna get upset if we say he got shot 'cause he was stealin', trespassin', hell, we could say anything. Nobody's gonna give a shit."

"Freeze."

Billy Leaps's voice came hard. It had authority. He had moved to within a few feet of the white men. He could smell the alcohol on their breaths now. It hung around them like a rotting cloud. They hadn't heard him approach. They turned quickly, to face the long, lethal barrel of his rifle.

The fat man with the fringe of blond hair did freeze. Fear ran over his face. His glands spewed sweat over every inch of his exposed skin. His belly shook visibly, quivering inside the worn denim.

The other one was cooler. Cooler, because he held a rifle too.

Good, thought Billy Leaps. *Real good. Maybe you'll do it for me, asshole. Maybe you'll give me my chance.*

"What the fuck are you doing here?" the man with the twenty-two demanded. His voice was haughty. It was the voice bigoted white men always used with Indians. Billy Leaps always wondered where they learned it. If their mothers taught them. If they picked it up from their friends. Or if it just came natural.

Billy Leaps didn't answer right away. He caught the man's eyes and stared into them. When he did speak, his voice had the same military authority as before. "I'm here," he said, "because I want to know what right you have to beat that boy."

The two men were momentarily baffled. The voice was harsh, demanding, but the question itself was almost casual. And this Indian, still holding the rifle on them, was smiling. They also saw that the Indian exchanged a glance with the boy, a moment's glance. The boy understood something, but the two white men didn't know what that glance meant. It was almost as if the Indian and the boy already knew each other. A father and a son could exchange such a look if they spent weekends hunting together every autumn—it was that sure and intimate.

Billy Leaps's look had been instinctive. It meant, *It's gonna be okay.* The boy had understood. The tears were drying on his cheeks.

Billy Leaps looked at the two white men with disgust and anger and loathing. He knew what he was going to do. He had no choice now, after he had seen them torture the boy, after he had heard their intention of killing him. He knew exactly how it was going to happen, and that was what his puzzling smile was all about. He'd pretend it was just like the Corps. Just a little training exercise in the Corps. And better than stalking woodchucks any old day.

The boy bound to the tree began to sag against his ropes. It looked as if he were about to pass out. The wound in his chest was possibly more serious than he had imagined, thought Billy Leaps. Maybe a lung had been punctured, and the boy was bleeding internally.

"Hold on," said Billy, making a slight movement in the boy's direction.

The white man with the rifle thought the Indian a fool— he had nearly turned his back on an armed man. *Well, Jesus,* thought Joe, *I'm the fool if I don't take the chance to rid the welfare department of two goddamn Indians right now.* He lifted his twenty-two and began to aim.

He didn't even see what happened.

He didn't see the Indian turn. Billy Leaps was just there, and so was the barrel of the rifle, aimed right for him. The shot came quickly, from three feet away.

The twenty-two was knocked aside, into the dense brush surrounding the clearing.

Joe himself went the other way. About ten feet the other way, straight through the air.

The echo of the rifle shot died away, and only then did the fat man in the stretched denim overalls begin to scream. One long yell of terror.

He had never seen this before. He had never known combat. He had never seen his best friend turned into a couple of hundred pounds of meat. But there it was. Joe's sternum was gone, just gone. His lungs were pulp, so there was not even a scream. It looked as if someone had just stood over him and scooped out his chest with a sharp-pointed spade—about three hefty scoops worth—and tossed the gore nonchalantly over his shoulder.

The fat man's face was wet, and when he reached up to wipe it, he found that he was bringing away little scraps of bloody flesh. Little scraps of his friend. He couldn't help, in his shock, but turn and look at the corpse. Joe lay on the ground, and in the middle of his red flannel shirt, there was nothing but a big hole, with shredded, burned edges. Blood was seeping into it, and some reddish-purple organ slid out of the lower part of Joe's belly into the cavity with a liquid *plop*.

The fat man started to cry. Not silently, manfully, like the boy, but with hysterical gulpings. His were the cries of a slothful man who has seen death in its naked, most violent form. Raw, grisly, sudden, unexpected. It wasn't death that looked like sleep, the way his brother had looked when he died, in the hospital. Not even the way death looked when you passed a highway accident, and saw some wife and mother sprawled on the roadside with a little pool of ketchupy-looking blood under her head. Joe wasn't even Joe anymore. He was just a slab of meat with a big hole in the middle, and somebody had put a mask on it, and the mask looked like Joe's face. The fat man was still crying and staring at his friend's corpse when he heard Billy Leaps move. The fat man turned. He knew there was a new bullet in the chamber. Even with the evidence behind him, the fat man did not yet realize that the bullet was for him.

Billy Leaps looked at the fat man and saw the knowledge of death come into his eyes. It had been a long time since Billy had seen that. And it was the same in every man.

Pale terror passed over the fat man's face. His legs trembled and collapsed behind him. He fell on his hands and knees.

"Oh, no, please no," whispered the fat man. He glanced at the Indian boy still bound to the tree. Had he beat the boy? If he had, it seemed years ago. And that was just a beating. He had just wanted to teach the boy a lesson. Even if the boy had died. That was nothing. It had meant nothing. It would have been something that took up an hour or so in the middle of a Sunday afternoon that was like every other Sunday afternoon. Still, the fat man could not make the connection between the Indian boy bound to the tree and his own death as it stared out at him from the barrel of Billy Leaps's rifle. He would die, and spend eternity, with that equation unsolved.

Billy Leaps moved forward slightly. This was a different kind of kill. He didn't have to protect himself against this one. The other had given him the excuse he needed. The other one had lifted a weapon against Billy Leaps. This one was just a witness, and wasn't that a shame.

The fat man, however, suddenly found his movements commanded by instinct. Survival comes out in even the lowest forms of animal life. A rat will attack a man if it's backed into a corner. A squirrel will lunge at a fox if death is very close. Even this fat man would try to survive in the face of his obvious doom.

Beeker could see it coming. The fear didn't leave the fat man's face. It was too deeply entrenched to go away. But there was a movement, a stiffening that was almost a spasm. The man had a knife in his pocket, a hunting knife. Terror still filling his eyes like blinding tears, he reached for it. He lifted it up and thrust it forward in his shaking hand. He tried to threaten the Cherokee.

Beeker just looked at him. The man remained on his knees. The knife waved aimlessly in front of him. He wept, without a trace of manhood left him. Instinct brought the knife out of the fat man's pocket, but it stopped there.

Billy Leaps pressed the enormous barrel of the rifle against the man's forehead. He held it there a moment, gauging his own feelings. It was easy, that's all; this was the easiest thing in the world to do. "Die, you bastard," he murmured, and pulled the trigger.

The fat man had tried to duck at the last moment. Billy Leaps could have compensated, but he knew that he wouldn't have to. The whole top of the fat man's head was blown away. It seemed to disintegrate, to vaporize. The fat man fell backward on the still-charred floor of the burned forest. What was left of his brain slopped out of his skull, like thin gruel spills out of a bowl. In the chill air it was smoking with heat.

Billy Leaps looked at the corpses of the two men he had just killed. He had wondered what it would be like. To see corpses after all these years. To know that if not for him the corpses would still be walking about on two legs, still guzzling beer, still pissing beer, still making bad jokes, and still laughing at them. To know that because of him, and what he did, those two men were rotting carcasses on the bare ground, drawing flies to their seeping blood and beginning to infect the air with the stench of death.

Even in the crisp air of a Louisiana winter, he could smell it. And it didn't bother him.

Years out of the service, years in "civilization," hadn't made any difference. He could kill. He could look on the result of his killing without revulsion or remorse. He had been trained not to care, and the training had held. He didn't care now.

These reflections took only an instant. Then he remembered the boy and turned to him. He expected to see that fear and defiance still in the youngster's face. He would be repulsed, horrified by the deaths. Probably the boy would fear Billy Leaps, as author of those merciless killings.

The boy was looking at him. His expression seemed composed of a single emotion: trust.

Billy went behind the tree and began untying the knots of the rope. He began at the neck. Swiftly all three ropes were loosened and fell in a heap at the boy's feet.

When Billy came back around the tree, the boy—his body obviously still wracked with the pain of the injuries to his ribs and his face—was moving uncertainly across the clearing.

Billy Leaps watched.

With difficulty the boy knelt on the bare ground. He retrieved the two pieces of .308 brass from Billy Leaps's rifle. Then he stood. He rolled the two pieces of yellow metal around in the palm of his hand. He put them into his pocket. Then he went and he stood over the corpse of the fat man. The corpse wasn't a pleasant sight. The top of his head was gone. One eye was open and staring; the other was merely red pulp. The mouth sagged, and inside was a wallow of blood. There was a stink from the sudden loosening of the fat man's sphincter at the instant of death.

The boy went and stood before the other corpse and looked at it as well. He neither hurried nor lingered.

Only then did he turn and look at Billy Leaps. The boy rubbed a swatch of drying blood from his cheek. He stared at Billy Leaps and tentatively used sign language. Billy Leaps was able to understand him. He had learned it as a teacher at the academy.

I am mute, the boy said.

"Are you deaf?" The boy shook his head. "You're injured," said Billy Leaps. "Rest. Sit down."

The boy seemed ready to argue, but couldn't. The pain was too great. Instead he continued to use his rope-burnt hands to communicate. *You are a great warrior.* He spelled out *warrior* letter by letter.

"I'm not a warrior, kid. Not like that."

Yes. You are a warrior. Just like the old days. Just like the old people. I have never met a warrior before.

"I am not a warrior. I killed those men because they were evil. Because they would have killed you. They would have killed an Indian boy. What tribe are you? Are you Cherokee?"

Billy Leaps was certain the answer would be no. He would be a Creek, or a Chickasaw.

Yes, the boy replied. *I am Cherokee. Thank you, Warrior.*

"Sit down by that tree," said Billy Leaps.

In an effort to obey instantly, the boy moved so quickly that pain overtook him and he staggered.

"Take it easy," said Billy Leaps. "Easy."

The boy walked slowly toward the tree to which he had been bound. He lowered himself carefully to the ground, lifting one side higher than the other so as to render the fractured rib as painless as possible.

"Listen to me," said Billy Leaps. The boy slowly raised his eyes. "I could get you to a doctor right now, but I'd have to leave these bodies. If you can hold out, I'd like to take the time to bury them right now. I've got a shovel in my pickup. Which will it be?"

The boy raised one hand and pointed at the two corpses.

Billy Leaps nodded. He said nothing to the boy. He turned on his heel and disappeared into the forest. A quarter of an hour later he returned with the shovel.

"When these bodies are buried," said Billy Leaps, "this will become a secret between you and me."

The boy's reply was to reach into his pocket and retrieve the two shells. He clutched them in his hand and pressed them against his injured chest. He winced with the pain that single movement caused him. *Secret*, he signed.

Billy Leaps looked at the boy and saw himself twenty years before. The same determination, the same coldness, the same alienation from all that was around him. Billy Leaps had already been like that even before he had gone into the Corps, before he had seen Vietnam. And now? Nothing had changed. He looked at the two bodies that lay between him and the boy. The corpses of the defeated enemy. The war Billy Leaps had fought so much earlier in his life had never really ended. And now he knew for certain that it never would.

He began to dig in the soft earth of the forest. He first marked off a long rectangle with the point of his spade near the corpse of the larger man and well away from the trees and their complicated root systems. He began to dig, and it soon became apparent that digging graves was much harder work than providing the corpses to fill them.

The sun was bright, and the labor was hard. Billy Leaps soon lost the sense of any chill in the air. He stripped off his layered shirts and worked half-naked, his skin gleaming with sweat and his muscles sharpened by the effort of his rhythmic, unceasing shoveling.

The boy sat mutely by. He was not able to move without pain, and so he sat perfectly still, only now and then raising one hand to his face to staunch a new flow of blood from his broken nose. Whenever Billy glanced up, he found the boy's eyes upon him. As he worked, Billy Leaps thought of the boy he had been.

A wretched twenty-acre farm over the state line in Oklahoma. No running water, and only a few naked light bulbs. Alone with his grandmother, a full-blooded Cherokee, who had raised him after Billy Leaps's mother—the bitch—had given into the bottle and found she loved it more than her own son.

His grandmother was a somber old woman steeped in a bitterness and a hatred that only a Cherokee could have sustained through eight decades without turning brittle and white. Twice-raped, she called her tribe: driven from their ancestral lands by ravenous White America, herded onto a desolate Oklahoma reservation, and forced to restructure their society and manner of living. And then to have that stolen as well when their bleak plains turned out to be the site of the liquid black gold, oil. White men threw up prim wooden churches wherever they went, but money was the only god they worshipped in their hearts.

So even this second home had been taken from them. What little dignity they had retained was swallowed in a repetitive cycle of poverty. It stole the health of the children and the pride of the adults, leading the fathers and mothers to drink and disgrace and self-hatred. These unhappy homes of the twice dispossessed became the real schools of each succeeding generation of Cherokee.

Against that dire background, and to some extent part of it, stood Billy Leaps's grandmother. She told tales of a once-proud people, a nation of warriors, the ancestors both of Billy Leaps and the injured boy who stoically rested his battered body against the tree to which he had been roped. The Cherokee were warriors with gifts and drives and abilities unknown, except to themselves, and to the tribes against whom they had warred. They had been conquerors, feared and honored.

The stories that Billy Leaps's grandmother had told were not legends, they were history. He knew that as he listened to her, cross-legged on the bare cabin floor. She knew what had happened at the very beginning of their race. Her knowledge went from those misty times when there was not even the knowledge that this was a continent. There was only the world which belonged to the Cherokee, and there were the other, inferior tribes, who kept their own tiny dominions by

Cherokee sufferance. Her tales ended only yesterday. But these latter stories were full of a despairing anger, a hopeless dignity, a proud suffering. They ended with the story of Billy's own father, a full-blooded Cherokee, who had died with a communist bullet in his warrior's belly in a foreign place called Korea.

Billy Leaps's grandmother had cared for him, cared for him in a way no one had before, and in a way no one would ever care for him again. Yet he knew that she had never forgiven him. She had never forgiven him for having a white mother. He saw her pain every time she looked into his blue eyes, the despicable reminder of his father's indiscretion with a white woman. It was her consolation that the line of a warrior was through the father, the man. Billy was certainly his father's son. She told him that often enough. She tried not to judge the boy by his mother, and Billy tried not to condemn his grandmother when she failed.

He was silent when she talked of his father's death. She was bitter that he had fallen on foreign ground, ground that meant nothing to her, or to the tribe. *Why was a real warrior on such a battlefield as that anyway?* she'd demand of Billy with sudden vehemence. The warrior was a trained man, a man of nobility and pride. He had no business trying to kill with the crude weapons of the Europeans. Such weapons brought no honor to the killer, and afforded no dignity to his victims. A battleground should be more than a slaughtering house; it was the field on which two nations, two tribes, and finally, two men, judged each other's prowess and honor. Where a man saw into the eyes of the man he would kill. Where a man about to die saw his death in the gaze, in the hand, in the practiced movement and the sanctified weapon of the warrior who was greater than he. Where was the nobility in a war fought with tanks and airplanes? In such a war, a fighter neither saw his enemy's face, nor was he present to hear his victim's expiring breath.

But Billy Leaps did not agree with his grandmother here. That had been his father's way, and Billy never forgot it. Billy knew his father had died an honorable death, and it did not matter that the name of the place was Hill 914, and that Hill 914 meant nothing at all, not even to the Koreans. Billy's father had died a warrior, a Cherokee warrior. He had chosen a quick, hero's death on Hill 914, rather than a slow termination in the taverns of eastern Oklahoma, swilling cheap whiskey and screwing cheap women.

So when he graduated high school and turned eighteen the following summer, there was only one thing for Billy Leaps to do. He went to Tulsa and found the Marine Corps recruiter. He enlisted. He only told his grandmother he was going to work the potato harvest in Arkansas, the way he had done the summer before. But he went to boot camp instead, at Lejeune in North Carolina, and when he returned to his grandmother's shack, he was wearing the dress blues of the Marine Corps. He stood at attention on the sloping front porch, knocked once at the screen door, and called to her in Cherokee.

She rushed to the door. Not for the pleasure of seeing him again, but because she had detected the change in his very voice. She already knew what had happened before she saw him. She wailed, a Cherokee woman's wail. It was the wail for the dead. She fell to her knees in the doorway, with the screen door unopened between them. She clasped her arms above her head and rocked back and forth, moaning low.

That night, however, she gave him her blessing. But, she never again looked him directly in the face. He knew it was because of the blue eyes. She blamed them. He heard of her death one day before the battle of Khe Sanh. A passing farmer had seen her corpse lying in the earth beside the chicken coop. She had died of a heart attack while doing her early morning chores.

It seemed to Billy Leaps almost as if it were his grandmother's grave he was digging, here in the clearing in the Louisiana forest. She had been a small woman, she would have fit here easily. He had to dig a little more, though, for this grave would have to hide two large men. It had to be at least four feet deep. Less than that and dogs or some wild animal would dig them up again for carrion. After two hours Billy Leaps pushed the shovel into the mound of dirt beside the hole and lifted himself out.

He turned and looked at the boy.

The boy signed, *I wanted to help.*

"I know," said Billy Leaps. He showed no sign of exhaustion. He picked up the feet of the fat man and drew him over to the side of the grave. Then he kicked him in. He shoveled dirt in all around him, just enough to provide an even floor for the second corpse, and to fill up the air pockets. It was air pockets that caused the grave of an uncoffined corpse to sink. Then Billy Leaps dragged over the second corpse, turning his face from the buzzing swarm of flies that covered the gaping hole in the man's chest. He pushed him in as well. He tumbled face down on top of his friend. Till the Resurrection then, they'd lie there together, in a cold embrace between old friends. Picking up the twenty-two with one of his shirts, he tossed it atop the corpses and then filled up the grave again. He packed it repeatedly on the top, leaving a slightly rounded roof to the grave so that the next rain wouldn't leave too great a depression over the bodies. He covered the grave exactly as he'd been taught to disguise a sunken trap.

Anyone knowing that the two white men had disappeared in this part of the forest would have difficulty in finding them. And even if they did, there'd be no fingerprints, and no witnesses.

Except the boy, of course. And Billy Leaps knew that boy would die before he told.

The boy had risen from the tree. A shudder of pain passed

through him, and he would have fallen to the ground had not Billy Leaps caught him. The sudden movement after three hours of sitting with the broken rib had been a shock to the boy's system.

"I'm going to carry you to the truck," said Billy Leaps.

The boy made no reply, but it was apparent he could not have walked the distance.

"Can you hold this?" asked Billy, placing the handle of the shovel in the boy's hand.

Billy Leaps set off carefully into the forest. His truck was parked a quarter of a mile away on a logging track off one of the county highways. He said to the boy, "It's over. You'll be patched up and good as new." Then he added, "It would be all right to cry."

The boy's face was hidden in his shoulder, and Billy felt rather than saw the boy's response: No.

2

Billy Leaps sat on a straight-backed wooden chair in his cabin. It was a sparsely furnished house that sat almost exactly in the middle of the sixty-five acres of land that he owned in the backwoods of De Soto County in the northwestern part of Louisiana. He had built the cabin himself. It was solidly constructed of pine that Billy Leaps had felled himself. His intention from the beginning had always been to spend the rest of his life under this roof.

It was an old-fashioned plan for a house: a fair-sized rectangle divided into two unequal rooms. The smaller room contained Billy Leaps's single bed, a military-issue surplus wooden cot, and an old free-standing wardrobe that had belonged to his Cherokee grandmother. The larger room contained a table, a few chairs, an old sofa, and a large wood-burning stove that was employed both for heat and for cooking. At one end of the house was a gas range, a gas-powered refrigerator, and a kitchen sink. A little closetlike bathroom with a toilet and a shower was closed off from the rest of the room by a heavy green-baize curtain. Multicolored rugs, woven by his grandmother from scraps of cloth shredded from old clothes, were scattered over the plank floors.

Lying on the couch was the young boy. Bandages covered his broken nose and were wrapped snugly around his bare chest. What skin showed around the bandages was heavily discolored, a motley of yellow, green, black, and blue that showed like a contour map where he had been beaten. The boy had slept on Billy Leaps's couch for the past week, ever since he had been attacked in the forest.

"How long you gonna keep that kid?" the man across the table from Billy Leaps asked. He was staring at his hands as he expertly cut the white powder of nearly half a gram of cocaine on a mirror. The razor blade he used clinked against the glass.

"He can't move around much," replied Billy Leaps. He glanced at the boy. If the boy felt any discomfort or embarrassment at being talked about in the third person, none showed in his eyes. "Doctor figures another couple of weeks, at least. Then he can go to school. That long, I guess."

"Jesus, Beeker, I never expected to find a kid out here. I figured you saw enough of those shits at the academy. What about this one's parents?"

"Who knows? He got farmed out by the welfare department. I went to see the people." He paused. The boy's foster mother was just like his own had been. Married to the bottle. He saw it in an instant. She took in foster children because she wanted the state money to keep her in booze.

"And?"

"And I wasn't going to leave him there, Cowboy. That's all."

Cowboy's real name was Sherwood Hatcher, but hardly anybody remembered that, and Cowboy himself always had the feeling, when he was signing his name to something, that he was forging some stranger's signature. He was thirty-five. Five ten, that's medium height, but he weighed only a hundred and thirty pounds. In Vietnam he had been nearly twenty-five pounds heavier, but in Vietnam Cowboy hadn't done coke. In the years since then, cocaine had murdered Cowboy's appetite. It had promoted an almost constant stream of nervous activity in his wasting frame. He was thin now. His face was gaunt. He chewed a wad of tobacco while he cut the cocaine. Billy Leaps kept an aluminum bucket under the wood stove for Cowboy's visits. Cowboy's fair skin and blue eyes combined with his blond hair and white eyebrows made it look as if the sun had leached all the color out of him. Everywhere, even here in Billy Leaps's cabin, Cowboy wore a showy cowboy hat and mirrored sunglasses, as if to protect himself from further bleaching by the sun.

Cowboy loved western shirts. The one he had on now was dark green with ivory snap buttons. He always wore sharp-toed lizard-skin boots. They cost eight hundred dollars because he had them made up special in San Antonio.

Another indication of the money Cowboy could show off if he wanted to was outside the cabin, hidden in a large rambling building that from the outside looked like a ramshackle barn. From inside, however, without stalls or lofts, the barn looked much more like an airplane hangar. And that was what it was. It housed Cowboy's twin-engine Beechcraft. Cowboy was a pilot and had learned to fly when he was twelve, taking rough-and-ready lessons from his father, a barnstormer. Cowboy flew choppers in the war. Now he flew the Beechcraft for fun. And a great deal of profit.

Cowboy flew the Beechcraft from Texas or Louisiana southward. Over the Gulf of Mexico, to countries like Venezuela, Colombia, or Bolivia. And there he picked up his cargo. Sometimes it was a small compact cargo—cocaine. Sometimes it was a large light cargo—marijuana. Sometimes there were crates that were a great deal heavier, but Cowboy wasn't curious, and he never tried to find out what was inside those. He flew down from regular airports in Texas, Louisiana, or Arkansas, but on his return trip he always landed at Billy Leaps's farm. And always at night.

Cowboy had financed the building of a paved drive from the county road up to the barn of Billy Leaps's place. The road curved and twisted around stands of trees and oxbows of streams, but the last few hundred yards or so were perfectly straight and level with barren fields on either side. Yet the road was so narrow that even seen from the air it didn't look like a runway. Nobody but a fool would try to land on a strip that narrow. Or a man who stood to make a great deal of money if he could keep his comings and goings a secret. With no sweat Cowboy could land on a strip of pavement that was only six inches wider than his landing gear.

You had to be careful about this sort of thing. The government had reconnoitering planes flying all over the place looking for marijuana fields and moonshine whiskey stills. A runway on land owned by an Indian would look mighty suspicious to a government inspector. What Indian could afford a plane, or his own private landing field?

Billy Leaps didn't care that what Cowboy was doing was in flagrant violation of the law. There was a time when he would have. But the government who made the laws against cocaine was the same government that had treated the men returning from the Vietnam war like lepers. Cowboy had saved Billy Leaps's life more than once. If Cowboy hadn't done that, Billy Leaps wouldn't be here at all. So what did it matter if Billy Leaps was putting himself at risk for Cowboy's sake? Even if the danger of discovery had been twice as great, Billy Leaps would not have refused to help his friend.

Cowboy sat up. He was done with the meticulous rapping

of the razor on the mirror. He had carefully created two long lines of the white powder. From his wallet he took a crisp new twenty-dollar bill and rolled it tightly. He inserted one end of the tube into a nostril and inhaled sharply as he moved the other end up the first line of cocaine.

He sat back and sniffed deeply. Then he placed the tube in his other nostril and repeated the motion. He breathed in the cocaine in one long, quick motion. He sat up stiffly. He sniffed again. He reached into his pocket and brought out a small plastic vial with a spray attachment. Inside was water mixed with glycerine. The interior flesh of his nose had been so burnt by constant use of cocaine that it required this soothing lubrication after every inhalation.

A bright smile came over Cowboy's face as he put away the water and glycerine mixture. He laughed with his mouth. His light blue eyes were hidden behind the reflector lenses of his glasses, but Billy Leaps knew they were laughing too. "Oh, sweet Jesus." Cowboy clapped his hands in childish delight. "Thank you for cocaine! God, Beeker, how do you live without the stuff? How do you face that goddamn school every day without the help of Mother C?"

Billy Leaps just smiled. Cowboy always asked the same question, and there had never been an answer. There wouldn't be one now. After Vietnam, how did any man get through the endless succession of days? He just did. With cocaine, some of them. With liquor, others. With a kind of deliberate bandaging of the mind. Everything was a way of forgetting what they had gone through. Everything was a way of ignoring the hell they suffered now. Everything was a deliberate ignorance of how little was left to them, these men who had returned.

Cowboy laughed again. He looked over at the boy on the dilapidated sofa and laughed at the bandages that covered his nose. "Boy, that's what I'm gonna look like in another year or two. That's what's waiting for me!"

The boy laughed too, his bandaged chest convulsing with the effort.

Billy Leaps stood up from the table and went over to the cot. He put a hand on the boy's shoulder to calm him. "You want water? A Pepsi?"

No, the boy signed listlessly, *I'm fine.*

Billy Leaps went to the refrigerator and brought out two cans of beer. He gave one to Cowboy and opened the other for himself.

"So," said Cowboy, who became calm a few minutes after every ingestion of cocaine, "how's life, Beeker? Except for cleaning up after your new boarder here?"

He pulled the tab on the beer and guzzled a long pull of it.

"Nothing much, Cowboy. Work." He shrugged his shoulders. "This year at school is pretty much like the last. Managed to pull together a soccer team this year. First time for that. Kids are pretty good. Some of 'em. Some of 'em aren't."

"Rich kids," snorted Cowboy in disgust.

Billy Leaps laughed. "Don't hear you complaining much about having money."

"Money's great for a man, Beeker. Money'll pay for cocaine. Money'll get you a piece of ass. Money'll buy you land. But for a kid? Money's just corruption. It makes a boy soft."

Billy Leaps glanced at the boy on the sofa. "Hear that? Make you feel better that you've been poor all your life?"

"You really like coaching at that goddamn academy?" asked Cowboy. "I don't believe it. You got a boss, right?"

"The headmaster," said Billy Leaps.

"I don't see you much liking toadying to him," said Cowboy, "whoever the fuck the old bastard is. Right?"

"I've got my boys," said Billy Leaps stiffly. What Cowboy said rankled. He didn't like the school. He didn't like having to answer to the headmaster. Faculty meetings. Monthly reports. Conferences with parents. Being told to coddle the rich boys and punish the high spirits of the few boys he really did like. And all the boys were white. Lily-white. One black kid, and he was whiter than all the rest put together.

"Right," said Cowboy, "you got your boys. But what do you do for"—he glanced at the kid on the couch and grinned—"female companionship?"

The boy on the couch grinned back.

"What do you do for a piece of ass out here in the wilderness, Beeker?" Cowboy went on, more plainly, to show the boy that he wasn't holding back because of him.

"I've had enough of women for the time being," said Billy Leaps. "When the need comes up, I've got ways of filling it; that's not what I'm talking about. But companionship? Female companionship? I don't need that. Not anymore. I tried it twice, once in town, and once out here. First time, in town, *I* couldn't take it. Cable television and lawn mowers. Second time, out here, *she* couldn't take it. No bathtub with hot water, no deep freeze, and no telephone."

"I sort of liked your last wife," Cowboy mused. "What was her name? Alice?"

"Alicia."

"Hot piece of goods," said Cowboy, and winked at the boy.

"She wanted me to be an Elk," said Billy Leaps in remembered disgust. "'Cause the Elks were a step up from the VFW. She clawed at me. She hated this place. Listen, Cowboy, if I had been building this place on my own, I would have had just one big room; that's the way a man lives. But Alicia went on about privacy. Alicia would have had a twenty-room mansion if I could have built it. When I was building this place, she thought it was just for the weekends, for me going out hunting. She wouldn't believe me when I told her I wanted to live out here permanently. She didn't believe it till I moved our bed out here. She lasted for about two months. Then she left, and she took the fucking bed with her. She's living with a swimming pool salesman in Florida now. She won't marry him 'cause if she does, I won't have to pay her any more alimony."

"Good riddance," said Cowboy, laughing. "But she was still a hot piece of goods. The problem was, you married the bitch."

Billy Leaps smiled. Cowboy had gotten himself married at least six times—he had lost count—but he didn't have a single divorce to his credit. Cowboy wasn't stupid about this particular indulgence. He didn't get married too close to home. Louisiana, Arkansas, Texas, and Oklahoma were definitely out. In those states he was a bachelor. But Colombia, Guatemala, Mexico—why the hell not? Getting married was a joyful habit for Cowboy, but if his wives expected something more than a romantic honeymoon—well, that was their problem, and they could deal with it themselves.

Cowboy spat into the old metal pan on the floor and looked back at Billy Leaps. "But now you got a kid. You're as tied down as you ever were."

Billy Leaps smiled. He turned and looked at the youth. "I don't think he's going to ask me to join the Elks, though."

Cowboy laughed again, and so did the boy. But the boy's laughter had relief in it—Billy Leaps had never before admitted that the boy might stay longer than his injuries demanded. The boy grasped the fragment of hope and clung to it as tightly as he had to the shell casings he had retrieved from the floor of the forest clearing.

Cowboy talked more about business. He had come to the

cabin to claim his Beechcraft. He was off to Colombia. "Big time again, Beeker, big time. Got a lot of my own money riding on this one. I'm gonna get back tomorrow night, and by the weekend half the noses in New Orleans are gonna be desert dry."

"Be careful," said Billy Leaps.

"Piece of cake," Cowboy responded.

Fifteen minutes later, while Billy Leaps was preparing the simple dinner for himself and the boy, they heard the roar of the twin engines as the plane powered itself up from the paved road and lifted into the night sky, headed for Colombia.

3

It was two days later that the phone call came. It was early in the morning. Billy Leaps had just finished dressing for school and was waiting for his morning coffee to stop perking. The boy was taking a shower.

Billy Leaps answered the unusual ring. He got more wrong numbers than actual calls. "Yeah."

"Beeker! Beeker! How's my man? How's my main man?"

Every muscle in Billy Leaps's body tensed. He hadn't heard that voice in years, many years, not enough years. He didn't want to hear it now. His gut told him to hang up. He didn't.

"Beeker, you there?"

"Yeah."

He had last heard the voice in Vietnam, God what? seven, eight years ago. It belonged to Woodrow Wilson Parkes, a sickly-looking asshole of a CIA operative who had tried to use Billy Leaps and his men for his own private purposes in the middle of the fucking war. Billy Leaps had learned the hard way that Parkes wasn't to be trusted. The voice hadn't changed, and Billy Leaps suspected that nothing else had either. Parkes wasn't to be trusted now.

"I hear about you, Beeker. Hear you're doing fine down there, just fine. Shreveport's not my idea of a hot city, but goddamn, if you grew up around there, I guess you can do all right for yourself. I hear those Southern belles got the tightest boxes in the continental states, that true, Beeker? You getting it squeezed a lot, Beeker?"

Parkes must be what—fifty-five, fifty-six now, thought Beeker, and he still talks like a goddamn high school locker room jock.

Beeker didn't answer. With a man like Parkes it was best to say as little as possible. But Beeker was making a mistake just by listening. His gut told him that. His gut said, *Hang up, Beeker. Hang up on the fool. And then tear out the goddamn telephone.*

"Look, Beeker, I got to be serious with you. I got this outfit up in D.C. Called Prometheus. It's an operation I got together with the help of some other guys. You know what I mean? I got friends who helped set me up in business."

The CIA worked through an elaborate series of fake business facades, especially when it wanted to accomplish something that Congress and its nit-picking committees wouldn't like if they found out about it. Money got channeled, money got squandered, money got poured into the pockets of men like Parkes. And men like Parkes then went out and pulled stupid college boy stunts that generally turned into an embarrassment for everybody.

"You listening to me, Beeker? We're seen as being freelance, private security, that sort of thing. But you know . . ."

Tricks, tricks, it was all of it tricks. They had tried their elaborate schemes in Vietnam, and—give 'em credit—the CIA had played all its little games to the hilt. There was one problem. The North Vietnamese weren't playing a game. They had one goal in the war, and that was to win. The CIA figured it could afford to lose a couple of the games, so it ended up losing them all when the North Vietnamese took control of the whole goddamn board. And now Parkes was back in it again, working a fake security business and gearing up to do a little of the Agency's dirty work.

"I got something, Beeker." Parkes's voice was lower now. Conspiratorial. He was luring Billy Leaps into his plan. "And it's hot, Beeker, really hot. As soon as I heard about it, I knew you'd want to be in on it."

"I don't want to be involved in nothing," Billy Leaps replied quickly, coldly. "Nothing involving you."

"Beeker, we know where Gougelmann is."

Billy Leaps froze. "Sure," he said after a minute. "We all do. He's six feet under, in San Diego. Dead and buried, and his wife doesn't send Christmas cards anymore since she got married again."

It was a mistake to have said that, Billy Leaps knew. Because he already knew what Parkes was going to say.

"You know better than to trust a headstone, Beeker. The gooks don't turn over real bodies. Just bits and pieces, Beeker, little bits and pieces. And those bits and pieces in Gougelmann's grave don't add up to Gougelmann."

Emotions played havoc in Billy Leaps's mind. He wanted desperately to demand *Where is he then?* But he didn't. He wanted Parkes to play his whole hand. Every card laid out on the table.

He might as well have asked his question, because Parkes answered it in the same low, conspiratorial voice as before.

"*Laos*," he hissed over the telephone. "They still got him, Beeker. They still got Gougelmann. And we can confirm seventeen others."

Seventeen others! In a communist jail in Laos. Jail—it

31

wouldn't be a jail. It would be a pen. A hole in the ground. Gougelmann, and seventeen others. Billy Leaps thought. What hell had those men gone through in Laos in the last eight years? Eight years with the gooks. He tried to say to himself that Parkes was lying. He tried to think of Gougelmann rotting in the grave in the San Diego cemetery, just bones now, disconnected bones lying on a satin cushion. But all he could think of was Gougelmann, his friend, just bones with a little connecting flesh, eighty-five pounds, in a pen in the jungles of Laos, burnt and tortured and beaten and starved for eight long years. In eight years Billy Leaps had had two wives, three jobs, four pickups. In the same eight years Gougelmann had had the same single day of imprisonment, humiliation, and torture repeated three thousand times.

"Why the hell are you telling me?" Beeker demanded. He had meant his voice to be hard. It wasn't. It revealed his anger, his concern, to Parkes.

"I need you, Beeker. You and your men. I want your team back. And I want you to get Gougelmann out of there."

Beeker said nothing, but he couldn't keep the words out of his mind. *The Team.* The Black Berets they had called themselves. An interservice collection of the bravest—and insanest—fighters that had existed in Vietnam. They had done the work no one else would do. They had followed orders like they were the ten commandments, graven on goddamn stone by the finger of God. Their talents had been used to the hilt, and occasionally their talents had been abused to the hilt, but they had been Beeker's men—and that team was the greatest accomplishment of Beeker's life. He had created the most celebrated, most feared, most vicious, most hated group of Black Berets in the whole goddamn lurching history of America's war in Asia. *The Team.*

Parkes said, almost casually, "You can imagine what it's been like for him. When you go to that school today, and you deal with those rich kids and teach 'em how to swing on parallel bars, and later on tonight when you punch a little pussy after you've had a steak dinner and a couple of drinks, you think about Gougelmann, and you think what *his* day must have been like."

Goddamn Parkes could read minds. Beeker made his decision. His gut churned.

"It's been years, Parkes. Years. I don't even know where they are." He couldn't bring himself to give in yet.

But he had opened the door for Parkes, and Parkes walked right in.

"I got their addresses. You still see Cowboy. Help him out, too, don't you, Beeker?" Parkes laughed, and Billy Leaps felt a slight chill of fear, not for himself, but for Cowboy, who had had no idea that his operation was not a total secret.

"Harry's in Chicago, got a bar called Harry's Place on the South Side. Real original, hunh? Harry's Place. Rosie's in Newark, working at Newark Memorial, in the burn clinic. Applebaum—"

"Forget that one," Billy Leaps broke in. "Just forget that crazy son-of-a-bitch is even alive."

"—Applebaum is in St. Louis, working for an outfit called Dominion Construction. That's funny, hunh? Applebaum working for a *builder*. It's the old team, Beeker, and if you call, they'll show up. You know it."

Beeker didn't answer. Parkes was right, and they both knew it. Even though, except for Cowboy, Beeker hadn't seen or spoken or heard from his men since the evacuation of Saigon. Twenty-ninth of April, '75. But they'd come. If he called.

Parkes was laughing again. "You got swamps down there, right? Down in Louisiana. But you haven't got jungle. Not real jungle. Missed it, Beeker? You and your boys? You missed the jungle? Hey, you take the devil out of hell and stick him up in heaven, and what happens? He gets homesick for fire and brimstone. And that's what it is, isn't it?"

Parkes's laughter turned into a choking fit before it finally died away.

"I still haven't said yes," Beeker pointed out. "I still haven't heard terms."

"I'm generous. I'm real generous. There's gonna be money in it. Fifty grand to start, and that's up front. All your expenses, up front. And fifty more when you get back."

"For five men? A hundred thousand dollars? That's not exactly generous. Not for what you're asking us to do."

"You'd do it for nothing," said Parkes in a low voice. "For Gougelmann. So don't try to shit me. You'd fucking pay me for the fucking map I've got. With X marks the spot on that poor bastard Gougelmann's head."

Parkes was right again.

Parkes's tone became jovial again, as quickly as a moment before it had gone sour. "Twenty thousand apiece. Not one of you fuckers, except for Cowboy, of course, makes that in a fucking year. Not one of you. Beeker, you make what, say, eighteen-five . . ."

Beeker's salary had been raised to eighteen-five exactly only the month before. Parkes was showing off his intelligence-gathering service. He was proving that he was still intimately connected with the CIA.

". . . so twenty thousand for a few months' work isn't so bad. And you get to clear your conscience to boot."

"My conscience doesn't need clearing, Parkes."

"'Course not, 'course it doesn't. Hell, it wasn't your fault Gougelmann got left behind to wither and rot in a hole in the ground in Laos. Not your fault."

No, for damn sure, it wasn't Beeker's fault. But it was Beeker's responsibility to get him out of that hellhole.

Beeker said to Parkes, "Let me think about it."

"You think about all you want. Prometheus Enterprises will be wiring ten thousand into your account this morning. That's for first expenses."

"I haven't said yes," said Beeker, angrily.

"Sure, sure," said Parkes. "But you will."

And Beeker knew that Parkes was right.

Billy Leaps hung up the telephone. When he turned around, he found the boy sitting on the couch, already dressed, staring up at him. Billy Leaps hadn't heard the boy come out of the shower. The boy asked no question. Billy Leaps said nothing about the call.

He drank his coffee and drove to school. For the past six years William Beeker had been head of athletics at the small and exclusive Shreveport Academy for Young Men. He handled the administration of all the athletic teams, he ran the gymnasium, he taught all the athletic classes, he gave sex instruction, and once or twice a year he was called in to cane a boy. If Mr. William Beeker had had his way, half the boys attending the academy would have been caned twice a day until a little of their well-bred snottiness had been beaten out of them. The job gave Billy Leaps little personal satisfaction, but he had long ago realized that after Vietnam, nothing that came to him stateside would. The job paid decently, he was for the most part left alone, and he had his summers off. Three and a half months out of the year, Billy Leaps could live the way a man should live. Out in the forest. In a house of his own building. With his own thoughts for his company. That was sufficient reason for putting up with these rich, spoiled kids and a school administration that toadied to the boys' parents.

Billy Leaps drove a Chevy pickup. It was three years old, painted a dull red. He kept it in prime shape, washing it every Saturday afternoon whether it looked like it needed it or not. When he parked it in the faculty lot at the Shreveport Academy, it stuck out like a sore thumb.

Academy faculty and administration clung desperately to the meager amount of social and educational prestige the school enjoyed. They tried to play on it by driving Saabs and Volvos, even when this meant taking them all the way to New Orleans for even minor repairs. One of the more sporty types in the English department even drove a vintage MG, though Billy Leaps suspected that on the open road it probably couldn't even work up to the double-nickel speed limit.

He arrived every morning at the academy ahead of all the other instructors. Sometimes he even beat the janitors. He liked to work out on his own. He'd run two or three miles to warm up before his first class, outside if it was at all possible. Then limber up inside the gymnasium with a basketball or some of the weight-lifting equipment.

Billy Leaps was preoccupied this morning. He couldn't get the remembrance of that call from Parkes out of his mind. Parkes's voice rang in his ears. Gougelmann's face kept rising up before him. As he did every morning, he stripped down and put on a jock, gym shorts, and a sweat shirt, then white socks and running shoes. One good thing about being a phys ed instructor was you didn't have to wear a suit and tie—well, just for a weekly meeting mandatory for all instructors. Billy Leaps had one good shirt, one wool tie, one blue blazer, one pair of gray woolen slacks, and a pair of loafers that he kept in his office locker for just those occasions. After Billy Leaps had divorced his last wife, he had thrown away all the rest of his dress clothes. His wardrobe was a standing joke in the school, but Billy Leaps had long ago stopped caring what anybody thought of him.

He was just about to swing out of his office, onto the dirt track that would lead him down along the lake, when for the first time he noticed a plain white envelope on his desk. It bore his name, typed in all capital letters. The envelope was sealed and must have been laid there sometime the previous evening. He tore it open. Inside was a brief letter, signed by the headmaster. It terminated his contract. He was given no reason for the firing, and he was advised against considering any legal recourse. "In that case," the headmaster had written tersely, "you would find yourself and your reputation greatly compromised."

Billy Leaps felt one single explosion of anger, a single flash that illumined the headmaster's body after Billy Leaps got through with him. His head was beaten to a bloody pulp. His fingers were crushed, his wrists, elbows, and shoulders carefully broken. His legs twisted apart. And Billy Leaps would have gone further in his imagination—and in reality—had he not just as suddenly cooled.

Cooled to an iciness that was as sudden as his anger had been.

It was simple. Parkes was behind it.

Parkes had gotten to the headmaster. Maybe he had simply bribed the man to fire Beeker. Or provided him some trumped-up story with fabricated evidence about some unthinkable indiscretion. Maybe Parkes hadn't done anything except tell the headmaster a little of the truth about Beeker's work in Vietnam—how many men Beeker had killed, how many raids against communist villages and strongholds he had initiated, how many different ways Billy Leaps Beeker had devised for getting information out of a Vietcong prisoner.

It didn't matter how Parkes had done it. That was the weird thing. Beeker didn't care.

It was like Vietnam. He had been undercut by his command-ing officer once again, that was all. Parkes had done it eight years ago, nine years ago, ten years ago. He was doing it again. Parkes had already known that Beeker would take on the assignment, but he was making sure. He had done Beeker out of his job. He had also probably made it impossible for Beeker ever to find work in a school again. Beeker knew from the tone of the head-master's letter that there wouldn't be any recommendations.

Beeker didn't care.

It had already become part of the assignment.

The check for the next month's salary was in the envelope as well. Beeker pocketed that. He walked out of the office that had been his for the past six years. He didn't even take the clothes that were in his locker. He'd have no more need for a cotton shirt, a wool tie, a blue blazer, gray trousers, and oxblood loaf-ers. Not anymore.

He drove to the bank and deposited the check in his account. He didn't even ask whether the ten thousand dollars from Prometheus had arrived yet. It had probably been there yesterday. Before Parkes had made his call.

4

If Billy Leaps Beeker had had any doubts that Parkes was behind his being fired from the Shreveport Academy for Young Men, those doubts were dispelled two days later when Cowboy returned from his drug run to Colombia. This was the run in which Cowboy was to have set himself up. He was to have bought two kilos of pure cocaine with his own money—all cash, of course; small American bills. On the American market he would have realized a profit of nearly one thousand percent. For every dollar Cowboy had invested, he would have got back ten.

It didn't quite work out that way. He'd appeared at the tiny airfield in the hinterlands of mountainous Colombia; he'd handed over his worn leather bag stuffed with every dollar he could scrape together. It was nearly a third of a million dollars, representing what Cowboy had put together after more than fifty just such flights into Colombia and Venezuela and Ecuador on the other men's business.

"I was fucked, fucked royally," said Cowboy to Beeker, and spat a wad of only half chewed tobacco on the ground. "Like I was a high school kid who decided he was going to take on the

Cleveland Mafia." With the sharp-pointed toe of his lizard-skin boot, he kicked at the earth under his feet. "I cannot fucking believe it."

"What happened?"

"I land there. Usual place. Everything looks the same, right. Same guys. Same fucking pouch. So I open it, and there's the stuff. I open one of the bags, and I taste it. For that kind of shit, my tongue's as good as my nose. I can taste quality. And it's fine. It's great. It's the best shit I've ever had in my life. I can't hardly wait to get back to Houston and get it to my man. I'm just thinking how much I'm gonna give him, and how much I'm gonna keep myself. So I give them my money—it's every cent I got, remember, every fucking dime—and I get that coke, and I'm off."

Billy Leaps already knew the end of this story. And he knew that somewhere, at the bottom of it, Parkes had contrived it all. The beginning, the middle, and the end. And poor old Cowboy. Poor old Cowboy still didn't suspect a thing. The Beechcraft was back in its disguised hangar on Billy Leaps's farm. The two friends were walking up and down alongside the roadway that was Cowboy's landing strip. It was just after dusk. Billy Leaps let his friend go on.

"So I get to Houston, fucking Houston, and all I'm thinking is 'I'm a rich man, and I've got enough coke to last me the winter.' And I take the pouch to my friend. My friend's going to spread the stuff all over New Orleans. He takes the pouch and he looks inside and he takes out the bags and he opens the bags and you know what he does?"

"What?"

"He digs down deep," said Cowboy in disgust. "And you know what he finds? He finds those Colombian fuckers have put a bag inside the bag. And the bag inside the bag is filled with talcum powder. Looks the same, weighs the same, not the same. I'm not worth five million, I'm worth about fifty thousand. And fifty thousand is what I borrowed from my friend in the first place. So I pay him off in the coke, and you know what? He's real generous; he lends me enough bread to get some gas at the airport. He gives me a dollar so's I can buy me some tobacco down at the corner grocery store. And he's real nice to do that for me 'cause his delivery schedule just got interrupted. But he says maybe I ought to take me a little vacation. And it looks like I'm gonna have to. Don't it?"

Billy Leaps made no reply for a few minutes.

It didn't often get cold in Louisiana. It was going to be cold tonight. Cowboy folded his arms across his chest. He stamped his feet. He looked closely at his friend. Then he glanced back across the darkened pasture to the cabin. The light was on in the kitchen. Cowboy could see the boy moving about there, slowly, deliberately.

"Parkes," said Billy Leaps. It was a single word in the darkness.

Cowboy jumped. But that surprise showed that he knew instantly what Billy Leaps was talking about. Cowboy didn't have to be reminded who Parkes was.

"It was Parkes," Billy Leaps repeated. "He set you up."

Cowboy was incredulous. "No way. Hey, that fucker—"

"He wants the team together again," said the Indian. "And to make sure that we get together, he's burning our bridges. He just lost me my job."

Cowboy's sympathy, despite his own troubles, was instantaneous. "Hey, Leaps, I'm sorry—"

Billy Leaps shook his head, and continued: "And of the five of us, you were the only one who had any money. He just cleaned you out."

"That was the Mafia who—"

Billy Leaps shook his head. It was so dark Cowboy could scarcely make out the movement.

"That was those fuckers in Colombia did that to me," Cowboy continued to protest, but more weakly this time.

Billy Leaps shook his head again.

"Goddamn." Cowboy swore softly, took off his hat, and slapped it against his thigh repeatedly. "Why the hell does he want a reunion?"

The two men continued to walk, up and down, up and down the runway. The boy only once glanced out the window at them, but then he simply sat down at the table and waited for them to come inside again. Outside, in the cold and dark Louisiana night, Billy Leaps told Cowboy why the reunion was necessary.

"Gougelmann," whispered Cowboy. "Goddamn it, Beeker, you think Parkes is telling the truth? Gougelmann in Laos?"

"I don't know," said Beeker. "I don't know if he's lying or not. But I'm not gonna take the chance that he's telling the truth. Once in all these years. If Gougelmann is in there, we're going to get him out."

Cowboy stared up into the sky. He saw stars, millions of stars. There were no street lamps, no glow from some nearby city, no auto headlights to wash out the tiny flickering lamps that shone in the black Louisiana sky. "You're right," he said at last. "You're absolutely fucking right. It don't matter one bit if Parkes is lying or not. As long as we get ourselves over there again . . ."

5

Harry's Place didn't quite fit in. The bar, on a forgotten cross street of Chicago's South Side, was obviously trying to establish itself as an improvement over the rest of the neighborhood. The facade of the building had been sandblasted a few years back, and the city grime still hadn't completely taken over again. Its windows were clean and neatly painted with the name of the place. The neon sign that projected perpendicularly over the doorway wasn't as garish as the competitions' advertising on either side. It looked like a workingman's bar that was trying to be clean and neat and respectable. And that was exactly what it was.

It was lunchtime on a cold bleak Chicago day. There hadn't been snow or rain for a while, but this looked to be the last day that the skyful of scudding clouds would hang fire. The twenty-five men or so inside the bar, eating sandwiches and drinking Pabst out of bottles, complained loudly anytime someone came inside and failed to shut the door tightly behind him. The Chicago wind took advantage of every crack and cranny. Most of the customers were decent men, construction workers in the neighborhood temporarily on a project or maintenance men at the enormous Bell Telephone installation around the corner who had been eating lunch there for years, even a couple of men in suits and ties who liked the way Harry's cook put a sandwich together. But of course there were a few drunks too, the men who couldn't get through the day without downing five or six beers at noontime, or even earlier, and who kept their jobs only through the grace and protection of their unions. The unemployed came to Harry's Place too, drinking fewer beers and nursing them till they grew flat and warm in their hands and staggering out sometime after dark, to return home to their sullen, unhappy wives and resentful children.

The two men who had the dubious distinction of being the most faithful of the patrons of the bar had their own special stools at the front end of the bar, just out of the draught by the door. These two men talked to each other every day, inclining their heads slightly toward one another till they had developed a permanent list, telling jokes they had heard a hundred thousand times before, making the same complaints, formulating the same lies, running down the same list of dreams they had revealed to each other the day before. They felt, moreover, that their unfailing patronage of Harry's Place gave them the right to claim intimacy with Harry himself. They took turns buying for each other, and every half hour one or the other would raise his hand in the air and call out loudly, "Hey, Greek, get me and my buddy here a beer and a shot."

And after that, Harry the Greek came down to the end of the bar with two cold bottles of Pabst. No one ever spoke his name—Haralambos Georgeos Pappathanassiou. Even sober the patrons of the bar couldn't have recalled that. He kept a bottle of rye down there, right beside his two most faithful customers, knowing the two men could kill it in a day. Lately they had been starting on their second. Harry the Greek towered over the two listing drunks. He was six two. He weighed at least two twenty. No one knew anything about him except that his name was Harry, he owned Harry's Place, he lived in rooms above the bar, and that he had been in the military. Harry's Place was open six days a week, and Harry worked all six of those days. He was never absent on errands, he never took days off, he never got sick. He opened at ten in the morning, and he closed at ten at night. His clientele was working men. They drank hard, but they didn't drink late. Harry didn't open at all on Sunday.

Thick black hair curled out at the V at the neck in his shirt. It was obvious that the hair would have covered his entire neck and shot up into a full, thick black beard if he hadn't shaved it every day. Above the stubble-darkened cheeks were green eyes. When he stood behind the bar with nothing to do, he was stock-still, staring into nothing. The green eyes showed only a passive vacancy. When he was called to fill an order, when the telephone rang, when his cook came out to ask a question, or a liquor salesman came in at the front door, the vacant expression dissipated instantly and was overtaken by an expression of great sadness.

Every man in the bar knew that sadness. It was the realization that you only had one life and that that one life had gone off the track and would never get back on the track again. But there was a difference between Harry and his customers. His customers came and they drank at Harry's Place, and the sadness was drowned for a few hours, held down by Pabst and cheap rye. Harry didn't drink, not at all, or at least not in the bar. Maybe in the rooms upstairs, after the bar was closed, and he was alone. But not downstairs, and downstairs, all day long, the green eyes alternated between vacancy and sadness.

Harry had a smile. It didn't suggest friendliness or mirth or good fellowship. It was just a smile that every bartender had to have if he wanted to keep his place open. Nobody believed it, but Harry smiled all the same every time he put down a bottle of beer, or poured out a shot of whiskey. He smiled at the two lushes at the end of the bar as he set down the bottles of Pabst and topped off the empty jiggers with cheap rye.

Then the smile froze. The bottle shook in his hand. He put down the bottle of whiskey with such force that one of the jiggers spilled. The two drunks followed Harry's gaze. He was staring at the front door of the bar.

Two men stood there. One of them was tall, dark-complexioned. Not quite white. Indian maybe. Right, maybe an Indian. The other was a cowboy. With a cowboy hat, and cowboy boots, and a cowboy shirt, and goddamn aviator sunglasses with mirrored lenses.

One lush hit the other on the shoulder and cackled, "Hey, goddamn cowboy and Indian. Hey, Greek, you got a—"

But the Greek was already gone. He went back to the cooler and took out two more bottles of beer. They were Pabsts, from habit. He glanced at them and then replaced them and drew out two bottles of Heineken. The cowboy and the Indian took the bottles. The Greek nodded toward the back of the room. There was an empty table there. The three men sat down together.

The Greek looked at Billy Leaps and then at Cowboy. The smile that passed over his face was an honest one. "A long time, guys. A long time."

Cowboy reached over and clasped the Greek's shoulder. He moved the huge man back and forth on his chair a few times and smiled. Billy Leaps sat silently, not moving.

The Greek looked in back of him, at the men who were sitting at his bar. "This place is all I got now," he said, without emotion and without embarrassment. "Me and these assholes. This is my life."

Cowboy said, "No new wife?"

"Never," the Greek shot back with low savagery. The muscles at the corner of one eye twitched.

Cowboy, sensing danger, sat back and sipped his beer.

"What are you guys doing here?" asked Harry after a few moments in which he seemed to regain his calmness. "In Chicago? In this bar?"

"We came to get you," said Billy Leaps. It was the first he had spoken.

"Get me?"

"I'm putting the team together again."

"What? Like a high school reunion?" demanded the Greek.

"That's what *I* fucking said," said Cowboy. "Like a high school reunion."

Billy Leaps shook his head. "For real." It wasn't his way to say much. These were men who would be convinced with ten words, if they were the right ten words.

The Greek sat still.

"Hey, Greek!" one of his patrons called. "I got to get out of here." He stood at the bar and waved his money. Harry ignored him. The man shrugged, left the money on the bar, and went out with his friends, muttering.

"Combat?" Harry asked.

Billy Leaps nodded.

"Where?"

"Laos," said the Cherokee.

"Whose mission? CIA?"

Billy Leaps hesitated, but before he could frame a reply, the Greek shrugged. "Hell, I don't care whose mission it is. But listen, Beeker, I haven't done anything but tend bar for the last five years. You know what I got for a weapon? You know what I'm good with now? I'm good with a baseball bat that I keep down behind there." He waved his arm behind him at the bar. "I haven't held a gun in my hands since I reopened this place. I don't even know where my knives are." Harry brought his hands up from the table and looked at the beefy paws, as if seeing them for the first time. "All I've touched in five years is wasted drunks. How can I go back?"

"Greek!" shouted one of the drunks at the end of the bar. "Get your hairy ass over here and get us some beer."

"And some rye!" shouted his friend. "Or we're gonna pour it ourselves!"

"You happy?" asked Billy Leaps.

"Sure I'm happy," the Greek replied without hesitation. "Sure, after being in Nam with you guys, the five of us together, our lives depending on one another every day. After what we went through together, after what you did for me, and I did for you, sure I'm happy. Pushing booze and beer nuts to a bunch of assholes. Sitting up in those two rooms all by myself every night and all day Sunday. Sure, I fucking love it!"

The last was louder than anything else the Greek had said.

He stood up. He tore at the white apron he wore and ripped it off. He dragged it over his head and slammed it on the table.

"Beeker," he said, "they ruined me over there. Ruined me to do anything else in my whole entire fucking life. After Nam, how do I come back to this shit and make believe it all didn't happen? After Nam. I'm supposed to live a normal life? I'm supposed to listen to drunks crying in their beer about how they lost their job, or their seniority, or how they got a piece of black ass back in '74? After what I saw—" He stopped. "After what I've *done*, how can I just go on?"

"You have gone on," said Cowboy, looking around the bar.

Most of the patrons left after the lunch hour were glancing uneasily in their direction. They realized that this wasn't a group to be interrupted with calls for more beer. More had left, leaving their money on the bar next to the register or on the tables.

"This is fuck-all," said Harry contemptuously. "I've been dead, Cowboy. Standing up in my shoes, but I've been dead."

"We've all been dead. For eight years," said Billy Leaps. For a moment he looked into the Greek's eyes.

For a moment the Greek saw sadness that matched his own.

"That's why we're going back," said the Cherokee. "We're going back because we have to. There's nothing left for men like us except to go back."

Harry sat down again. "The five of us? Just like before? Great Christ, it'll—"

"Not the five of us," said Cowboy. "Not Applebaum. You and me and Beeker and Rosie. Not that crazy motherfucker Applebaum. He was born crazy."

Harry considered this. Cowboy was right, and Applebaum was crazy. Crazier than anybody Harry had ever known. But Applebaum had also been Harry's friend. You didn't choose your friends any more than you chose your face or the color of your skin. Friends just *were*, and Applebaum had been his friend. "We got to have Applebaum," Harry argued, looking at Cowboy. "He's great with the bombs. You know he is. He knows more about explosives than anybody in the whole goddamn world. It don't matter what our mission is, we'll end up needing him. It always worked with five, the five of us, and it's not gonna work now unless we have Applebaum. You don't want him 'cause he was a SEAL. And you were a goddamn Green Beret."

"You were a SEAL too," said Cowboy. "Besides, who gives a good goddamn anymore what kind of uniform we wore? We were there, and we were there together, and that's all that matters. You think you start talking in this place about SEALs and Berets, these guys are gonna even know what you're talking about? We don't want Applebaum 'cause Applebaum is a crazy fuckhead, and it's a wonder he didn't kill us all. After eight years I'm not giving him another chance at my skin."

The Greek said nothing. He knew Cowboy was right. He looked at Billy Leaps.

The Cherokee said, "No Applebaum."

That was the decision, and the Greek knew it. Billy Leaps had been his leader, he was his leader again. If Beeker said no Applebaum, then Applebaum wasn't going to be there. Even if it meant they all died because that crazy SEAL wasn't around.

Harry nodded once.

Billy Leaps told Harry the deal. The Greek reacted as both Beeker and Cowboy had. He was distrustful of Parkes, but that consideration was swallowed up by his eagerness to reestablish the team and to get back to the jungle. Privately, Harry thought that Gougelmann was long dead, rotted in his grave in San Diego, but he said nothing. He didn't care if it was a wild-goose chase or not.

By the time they had finished, nearly everyone in the bar had left. It was half-past two. Lunch hours were over, and the drunks who could have remained weren't getting served. Only the two resident lushes at the very front of the bar had stayed. They had grown resentful at being ignored for so long. One of them had leaned forward and retrieved the bottle of rye. They finished that off in fairly short order, lingering only on the last shot-glassful.

A few minutes later two more men came into the bar, steelworkers just getting off their staggered shift. "God," said one of 'em, "I need a beer." They looked around for Harry, and one of the resident lushes pointed at the table in the bar. While his friend disappeared into the men's room, the other steelworker went to the back of the bar, pushed Harry on the shoulder, and muttered loudly, "Come on, Greek, you gotta take care of me and my buddy. We can't wait all fucking day for a fucking beer."

The Greek looked up at him. All the loneliness and sadness was gone from his eyes. Anger had taken over. A furious anger that Cowboy hadn't seen on a man's face in eight years. Billy Leaps had seen it, though. In the rearview mirror of his pickup as he was driving away from the forest where he'd left two men dead. In his own eyes. There was no reason for Harry to feel anger toward this one particular man. All his customers talked to him that way. That part was different. Harry himself was different. And the new Harry wasn't taking any of that shit.

Harry stood up. He towered over the man. He took him by the lapels of his workshirt and lifted him bodily from the floor. Panic swept over the man's face. He had been coming to this bar for years. He had never seen rage on the Greek's face, just a pacific sorrow. But now the Greek's green eyes had come to life with a fury, and the man was being lifted up so that he could stare directly into them. The Greek's arms contracted and suddenly the man felt himself flying through the air. Just as suddenly he was flat on his back on a table. And he wasn't thinking about anything else for a long while.

His friend came out of the restroom while the bottles and glasses that had been overturned were still tinkling on the floor. He stared at the unconscious body of his friend. He came around the end of the bar and, without a moment's hesitation, started for Harry. His name was Harv, and he knew how to use his body. He had fought plenty of fights in this neighborhood and had no fear of the bar owner. He thought the Greek had just gone a little crazy. Maybe Harv would just hold him down a bit. Till the Greek's friends could calm him.

But the Greek wasn't frightened when the steelworker came on. He loved it! A big open smile broke out on his face. "Come on, Harv, come on, Harv," he said in a low voice, egging him on with his hands.

Cowboy let out a whoop of pleasure. "The real thing, Harry, the real thing!"

Harry lunged at the steelworker, taking him down with a leg sweep. The two of them fell to the floor with a crash. Their enormous entwined bulk overturned more tables and rolled over broken bottles and glasses. Harv the steelworker suddenly realized that he had misjudged entirely. This was not the kind of fight he had fought before, not on the South Side of Chicago, and not *anywhere*. He gave himself over to instinct. He had to. There was nothing else to do. The two men were immediately engaged in a battle that had no rules. No limitations. No restrictions. Fists slammed into guts. Knees slashed at groins. Elbows smashed against faces.

But there was no way that Harv was going to win this one. No way at all. In minutes Harry was straddling his chest. He held Harv's head in his hands, just above the neck, his thumbs pressing against Harv's Adam's apple. The Greek was pounding Harv's skull onto the hard wooden floor, still strewn with glass. Again and again the sound of bone smashing against wood echoed through the bar. The two drunks at the end of the bar watched for a few moments in horror and then eased off their stools and out of the door, hoping Harry would not notice.

Harry didn't notice. He was frozen, the only motion in his body, a small flick of his massive wrists that slammed the steelworker's head repeatedly against the oaken floor in an unvarying rhythm.

"Harry! Harry" Cowboy shouted. "Stop! He's out cold."

Harry didn't hear. He went on.

Billy Leaps went to Harry's side, dropped down on his haunches, hauled off, and slapped Harry across the face.

It might have knocked another man cold.

Harry's head snapped to the right, then slowly returned. He looked down at the man's head cradled in his hands, then dropped it with surprise. The steelworker's skull thudded against the blood-soaked floor.

"He's still breathing," said Cowboy, kneeling beside the steelworker with his hand on the man's chest.

Harry stayed straddled across Harv's heaving chest. "I could have killed him." There was no emotion in the words. "I could have killed him easy."

Billy Leaps only nodded.

Cowboy stood up. The two steelworkers were both unconscious. They were otherwise alone in the bar. Cowboy said, "We got to get going if we want to hit Newark tonight."

Harry went into the kitchen. He said to the cook, "Call an ambulance for those two guys. Then lock up. Take the money that's in the register and find yourself another job. Harry's Place is closing down. As of right now."

The Greek never looked back.

6

Roosevelt Boone just loved dead people. Really, they were so much easier to deal with than living folks. Rosie talked to dead people all the time, and he didn't get any of the flack from them that living people were always handing out. Dead people didn't say thank-you much, but they didn't talk back either. They certainly didn't talk about Vietnam and didn't make remarks about the color of your skin, and they had all learned the one great lesson of life.

The one great lesson of life was that survival was the only thing that mattered. The dead had learned the lesson by default, of course.

The lesson didn't do the dead much good anymore, and Rosie felt sorry for them. So he talked to them. Just the way he was talking to this white girl right now. The chart said her name was Sarah Martin and she was from Hackensack. Well, poor Sarah made the mistake of her life earlier in the evening. She got in the wrong car. It was the wrong car because the right car wouldn't have ended up smashed into the median rail on the Turnpike two miles south of the George Washington Bridge.

So Sarah Martin was dead. But that didn't mean she wasn't a useful member of society anymore. Hardly. Sarah Martin was making herself very useful right now, and Rosie was telling her thank-you on behalf of all the people she was going to help.

"Sarah," said Rosie in a low, lilting voice, the voice he sometimes used on young women who were very much alive and in his bed, "there are these kids down in the ER. Cutest little bunch of kids you'd ever want to see. Except they got burned, burned bad in this big fire over in East Orange. Tenement fire. And their mama is real upset. I saw her crying when I came in to work tonight. Saw her weeping her eyes out. But those kids are gonna be all right. Their mama is gonna be able to hug those children tight some day, all because of what you are gonna give 'em."

Rosie held a handful of small steel instruments. Some looked like Exacto blades, others like sickles, others like scalpels. He was an artist with them. Sarah Martin, just a little mangled, with a crushed arm and a broken neck and a face torn to ribbons with windshield shards, lay naked on the steel table under the harsh fluorescent lamps of the basement of Newark Memorial Hospital. With the instrument that looked like an Exacto blade, Rosie had drawn a long rectangle that started at her ankle and went up the inside of her leg to the very joint of her thigh. Then, with two more instruments—one of them a scalpel and the other the sicklelike piece—he gently loosened this long flap of skin from the musculature that had held it in place on Sarah Martin's leg for the last nineteen years. He was very quick and sure about his work, and when he was done, he said, "All right, Sarah, I'm gonna pull this now, and what I'm hoping is that you're going to make this real easy. We want one long piece. Sarah, you just think about those little burned babies up there, and you make this one easy for me."

He took a sterilized, polished stick and laid it at the narrow end of the rectangle of skin, just at the ankle. Then he carefully lifted up this end flap and wrapped it around the stick, holding it in place with one thick black finger. Starting with this, he very carefully rolled the rectangle of skin over the stick. It came off perfectly, and in a very few seconds Rosie was holding up a three-and-a-half-foot bandage made entirely of human flesh. Sarah Martin's flesh had been white—probably hadn't been out in the sun since summer—and the bandage was discolored only at the edges, where the scalpel had cut.

"Ohh," he cooed, carefully placing the bandage in a chemical bath that would preserve its suppleness for several hours more. "You did good, Sarah, you did real good. In another couple of hours those little black babies up there are all going to be wrapped up in your pretty white flesh." He chuckled. "Bet that wasn't how you thought you were going to end up the evening, was it, girl?—when you climbed in that Volkswagen with your boyfriend this afternoon. You thought you was going off for a hot night in the city, didn't you? Didn't know you were going to end up wrapping yourself around three little burned black babies, did you?"

He drew another rectangle along her leg, then another, and another. Then he did the other leg. Then he turned her over and began on her back. The legs were best because he could get the longest bandages. When Rosie was showing off, and he was almost always showing off, he could start at the nape of the neck and go all the way down to the ankle. Within an hour Sarah Martin looked a great deal worse than when she had been brought into the morgue. She had been peeled. By a sex maniac, it looked like, for the only parts of her that remained intact were the nipples on her tiny breasts and her sexual organs below. Her crushed arm and lolling neck and slivered face looked almost good in comparison.

"Oh, no," said Rosie, pulling the sheet over her and holding it up to speak to the girl one last time, "no open coffin for you, Sarah, sorry about that."

He was black as night, with deep brown eyes and an ugly, almost red scar running down the cheek on the left side of his head. In his left ear he wore a white ivory earring carved into the likeness of a grinning skull. The fluorescent lights of this room hidden behind the morgue proper made his skin look blacker than it was. It made the tiny skull in his ear shine, like a tiny warning beacon.

Roosevelt Boone just did not like living people. Whenever he had to deal with them, he seemed to get into trouble. If he hadn't been so good at his job, he would have been fired any number of times, but the director of Pathology and the director of the Burn Institute had always intervened. Who else would spend his whole workday peeling the skin of cadavers, rolling the bandages that were all that the severely burned could take next to their blistered flesh? So what if Rosie was a little strange and had a tendency to pick fights with security guards? The answer wasn't to get rid of Rosie; the answer was to tell those damn guards to stay out of his way.

Rosie could be charming too. If he wanted to. He usually only wanted to be charming to pretty nurses who could give him a good time, whose skin was black like his, and whose lips promised sweet kisses and whose behinds rose high in the air and lifted up skirts that covered the wonderful treasures of a woman. Rosie could be so very nice to a nurse who let him taste her beauty. But then there were the rumors about Rosie's temper that displayed itself when a nurse tried to be coy, or when she turned away at the last minute, unable to ignore the slight stench of death that hung about Rosie's hands.

A few nurses got into trouble because they couldn't believe that this nice-looking, happy-looking man, whose laughter boomed in the corridors of the hospital, could possibly be the one who peeled skin off cadavers and who had—only reportedly—turned on a few other girls with such fury. Rosie always seemed so pleasant, and his eyes when they turned on you were deeply brown and romantic. But every once in a while one of them would misjudge, and they'd find a new truth in those eyes.

What Rosie didn't expect was the three men who were standing in the doorway to his workroom. One moment he was looking down at Sarah Martin's lacerated face to try to figure out if she had been pretty or not, and the next moment he was staring into the eyes of men he hadn't seen in what?—seven, eight years. And on the other side of the world.

The tank beside him was filled with more than a dozen rolls of white skin. White skin to wrap up three little burned black babies.

"Rosie," said Beeker, "we got to go back."

"Yeah, all right."

That was it for Roosevelt Boone. He didn't ask any questions, because he didn't need to. He didn't hesitate, because he knew he'd end up saying yes. Beeker was the head of the team, even though the team hadn't existed for eight years, and if Beeker said they were to go back, then that was what the team was going to do. He looked around the starkly clean morgue where he had been working and wondered how many dead people he had talked to in all these years. Not as many as he had talked to in Nam. The only difference was that in Nam the dead were mostly outside. Here, they were all inside. And all things considered, that wasn't a hell of a lot of difference.

What they didn't know when they had given him this job in the hospital, and the director of Pathology had showed him what to do with the corpses that came in, was that Roosevelt Boone had done it before. He had had experience.

Rosie stared for a moment at Cowboy, and at the Greek, silently noting in their faces and their bodies the passage of the years. Then he looked at Beeker again, and instead of thinking of what had come between, he was carried back.

For one six-month period he and Beeker had had a routine together, often repeated. Rosie didn't remember now how the pattern had come about, whether it had been ordered, whether it developed naturally. He didn't remember the first time they did it, and he couldn't remember the last time either.

They called it "Hunting the Papa-San." They'd infiltrate a gook village where the people were supposed to be Cong, or hiding the Cong, or sympathetic to the Cong, or something. And they'd find the village headman. Always. And they'd get him to talk. Always.

One time Rosie did remember. They hadn't been out after information, but revenge. It was clear that a Green Beret team had been exposed to the Cong by the people of this one village. A good friend of Rosie's had been killed. Not sniped. Not slashed. Not blown to bits with a mine. Alexander had been wounded in the leg. He couldn't get away. Men from this village had come up and rammed an unpinned grenade up his asshole, then scattered. They stood behind trees and watched as Alexander exploded. Wondrously, Alexander had lived a minute longer. His own body had muffled the shrapnel. His body was torn apart below the waist. It just wasn't there, but Alexander had retained life and consciousness long enough to know what had been done to him. Rosie found his body, his head and trunk intact, his bloody hands clutching at the dried earth, his feet still inside his combat boots, and nothing at all in the middle but cooked bloody gobs of flesh and tatters of burned cloth. So Billy Leaps Beeker and Rosie had gone into the village, in dead of night, and found the headman of the place, and they had taken him out to the edge of a rice field.

The old man stood up straight in the light of the full moon. He was going to be a strong asshole and stand up to the enemy and die an honorable death and all that bullshit.

Rosie wasn't having any of that. He'd make the old man die with terror like his friend Alexander must have felt.

Beeker didn't try to hold back any of Rosie's fury. Rosie returned to the village and found the old man's son, a lazy seventeen-year-old who was trying to pass himself off as fourteen so that he wouldn't have to go fight, for either side.

Rosie had done to the old man's son exactly what he did to Sarah Martin. Except that the old man's son was still alive, and he protested. The young draft-dodger didn't like it when Rosie took his knife and cut out a long rectangle of flesh from his arm and then wound it tightly around his father's neck.

Thousands of years of torture and humiliation and occupation had left the Vietnamese almost oblivious to the idea of panic and disgust. But with that feel of his son's living skin around his neck, the old man shuddered and shut his eyes.

The young man died by slow degrees. The father seemed to die at the same pace, as more and more skin was draped over him.

"Kill him! Kill him!" the old man pleaded in Vietnamese. Roosevelt Boone continued his slow torture by the light of the moon, while Beeker, with his back turned to them, kept watch.

"He deserves it!" the old man argued, hoping by any means to hasten the death of his suffering son. "He killed the American soldier. It was he—"

Rosie stopped. He turned to the old man. Beeker looked back over his shoulder. "Your son killed the soldier with the hand grenade?"

The old man nodded. The flesh that was draped about him had already begun to rot in the hot, humid night.

Rosie shrugged. He turned back to the young man, who had fainted. Rosie slapped him awake.

"I want you to watch this," said Rosie.

He cut open the young man's pants. Then grasping his genitals in his great black paw, he severed them with one swift cut of his knife.

The young man gasped in horror. Blood poured out between his legs. He would die within a minute.

But before that minute had elapsed, the young man had seen his genitals stuffed down his father's throat, and he had seen the old man gag and choke to death on them.

Both corpses lay there on the edge of the rice field. The pools of their blood looked black in the moonlight. Rosie cut off the ears of father and son, pricked holes in the lobes, and threaded the ears on a loop of string. He tied the string around his neck with trembling fingers, and when he turned to Beeker, there were tears in his eyes. His friend Alexander had died. And Alexander was now avenged.

Billy Leaps only nodded. He understood.

Billy Leaps had witnessed the greatest savagery that Roosevelt Boone had been capable of, and he had nodded with understanding.

Neither of them had ever mentioned the incident again.

Rosie looked around the morgue. Sarah Martin's feet were sticking out from under the sheet. He grasped one of them, shook it affectionately, and said, "See you later, girl."

"Let's go," said Beeker.

7

The Beechcraft dove down onto the Louisiana field. The three passengers scarcely felt Cowboy's smooth landing as the plane's brakes took hold and slowed the craft. He taxied to the barn and pulled right in.

It was strange that the doors to the barn were open. The boy had evidently expected them. Beeker wondered how he knew they would be returning just when they did. Beeker would have called to give warning, but the boy, being mute, didn't answer the telephone.

They were all tired. It had been a long trip down from Newark, with a stopover in Raleigh for refueling. They climbed out of the plane and stretched. Rosie tossed out the little luggage they had brought, and Harry caught and set it down in a neat row.

"Nice place, Beeker," said Rosie, peering out from the open door of the plane at the well-kept fields and the modest house.

Billy Leaps waited for the boy to come out and was passingly surprised that he hadn't yet greeted them. He must have heard the engines. Probably he was shy around strangers.

Cowboy was pulling shut the doors of the barn. Suddenly an explosion ripped open the ground a few dozen yards away. The men were startled. Another explosion, closer.

Instincts revived, and they all four dropped to the ground.

"Incoming! Incoming!" Harry yelled, a nightmare of Vietnam suddenly playing itself out in the present.

A third explosion, still closer.

The expression of each of the four men was one of a grim determination to survive.

The boy, Billy Leaps thought, *they're going to hurt the boy.* He had new instincts in him now, ones more powerful than his own survival. He started running, crouched over, his arms held as though they were cradling a rifle, just like the old days. He got to the house and threw open the door, his eyes blazing, his muscles ready—but for what?

The boy was sitting on the sofa. Fear and confusion were written on his face. Sitting beside him on the couch, rocking back and forth in silent laughter, was a small weaselly-looking man with thinning blond hair. "Got you motherfuckers!" he shrieked. "Scared the shit out of you!"

He pointed down at four plungers on the floor in front of him. Wires connected all of them and snaked across the floor and out the back door of the cabin. Three had been depressed; the fourth was still up. Casually, the man pressed down the fourth plunger with his foot.

There was another massive explosion outside, this one nearer and louder than all the others.

"Applebaum!" Beeker demanded. "What the hell do you think you're doing?"

"I'm celebrating, Beeker! What does it look like? Oh, man, just think, we're going back. The five of us. Going back."

The other three men had entered the house.

They stood in shock together, just inside the doorway. They stared at Applebaum, who was shaking his head and choking on his own laughter.

It was the first time the five men had been together since the fall of Saigon. Since that spring day in '75 when the helicopters were taking off from the roof of the American Embassy.

Cowboy was the first to speak. "You miserable bastard. You crazy, miserable bastard."

Beeker just stared at Applebaum. Rosie went up to Beeker and put an arm around his shoulder. It was comforting for the moment, but Rosie was ready to turn it into a restraining hold if he had to.

It was only the Greek who responded to Applebaum without anger. "Goddamn, Marty! I should have known it was you!" Harry went across the room and put an arm around his Army pal. The two men clapped each other's shoulders.

"I ought to kill that crazy son-of-a-bitch," murmured Cowboy.

Rosie felt Billy Leaps relax. He released his hold. Billy Leaps went over to the boy, and ignoring the boisterous exchanges between Harry and Applebaum, he assured the boy it had been a practical joke. "Don't worry," he said. "It's okay. Were you scared?" He regretted the question as soon as he'd asked it. Obviously the kid had been terrified but would never have admitted his fear. What must he have thought?—this stranger coming in, setting up explosives, triggering them. "It's over. Don't worry about it. Applebaum's just sort of loco, and he does things like this every once in a while. Okay?" The boy shook his head, yes.

Then he held up his hands. For the first time Billy Leaps saw that the boy's hands had been tied together.

Beeker looked down. The boy's feet too.

He was glad of that. The boy had tried to stop Applebaum, and Applebaum had tied him up.

Applebaum didn't look like he could have handled the boy. He was much smaller than anybody else in the room. Only five seven. His hair had thinned since Beeker had seen him last. He was balding quickly, though there'd probably always be a fringe. His weepy blue eyes were framed by black, square-rimmed glasses. When Applebaum and Harry's almost adolescent glee at seeing each other again had subsided, Billy Leaps broke in. "Marty, how'd you find out about this?"

The blond man looked up at the Marine and said, "Parkes. Parkes found me in St. Louis and told me we were all getting together again and going back. He gave me a map, and I drove down this morning."

"Did he tell you about the mission?"

"Who the fuck cares?" Applebaum shrugged. "Just as long as we're together again. God, I missed all you guys. I've been working in demolition. And hey, I'm good. I'm the best. But goddamn it, it's not the same." He grinned wickedly. "Nobody gets hurt," he explained in a lower voice.

Cowboy glared at Billy Leaps. "I will not work with this crazy son-of-a-bitch."

"Oh come on, Cowboy," said Harry. "He's here, come on, we can use him. Did you see those explosions out there? They were great."

"They nearly blew my balls off," complained Rosie. "That's how great they were."

"He's not a human being," Cowboy spat.

"That's right," the little blond man agreed. "I ain't a human being. Nobody who's been a SEAL is a human being. We're fucking animals. *Animals.*" He tore open his shirt and shoved down the right sleeve. On his bicep was a tattoo, the colors new and bright. It was a grotesque rendering of a skull, blood dripping from its hollow sockets and bared teeth. Beneath the skull in large letters was the legend: I BRING DEATH. Applebaum's sinewy arm was so slender that the letters almost encircled it.

"Jesus Christ," sighed Rosie in disgust.

8

The fire was burning in the wood stove. The five men and the boy had finished their meal, and now everyone was sitting around silently. Thinking. Remembering. The reunion had forced them all to remember too much.

"What's it been for you?" Beeker asked. He was looking at Rosie, but the question was meant for them all.

Rosie waited a moment, then answered: "Weird. Like nothing I expected. I came back and there was my wife, the one I married just before I shipped out. She didn't even meet me at the plane. She was just waiting at home, and when I walked in the door, you know what she said? She said to me, 'How many women did you kill? How many children did you kill?' And then she walked out, and I never saw her again."

Rosie's words lingered. The burning wood crackled in the stove.

Billy Leaps spoke again. "I got that one a lot too. Women and children. Because that was what they saw on television. It made me crazy. It still does. They don't ask anymore, but when you say 'I was in Nam,' that's still what they're thinking. You can tell."

MICHAEL MCDOWELL AND JOHN PRESTON

"Right," said Cowboy. "They don't ask you what it's like to see your best friend get it from a bouncing betty. They don't ask you what it's like to hold your hands on somebody's belly so his guts will stay in till the medic gets there. They don't ask what it's like when you see a company of gook running up at you, every damn one of them praying to their god that you'll die."

Somehow, then, all the eyes in the room turned to Applebaum. Maybe because he was the craziest. Maybe because they all wondered if he had somehow not suffered what they had suffered just because he *was* so crazy.

"When I got back," said Applebaum, his eyes becoming shifty, and gleaming red in the firelight, "Mama was ashamed of me. She never even told her friends that I was over there, 'cause she was so ashamed of me. She told her friends I was a clerk in San Diego. Mama didn't think I was a hero 'cause I went to Nam. Mama thought I was a piece of shit."

"We were all treated like shit when we got back," said the Greek. "The worst thing was that nobody treated you straight. You couldn't get away from the bullshit. When we were over there, it was hell. A rotten, stinking jungle hell, and it was a miracle none of us got killed. But you know what was great about it? We were all straight with one another. That's what was great. But we come back, and what happens? Everybody's playing a game, a fucking game. I mean, over there we had to be friends, didn't we? Here was old Marty"—the Greek waved his hand toward Applebaum, who was sitting nearby, staring into the fire—"and Marty's a crazy son-of-a-bitch, and everybody knows it, but goddamn, Marty was my buddy. And Marty saved my ass twenty times, and I saved his ass twenty times, and that's what it was like over there. But I get back here, and what have I got? I got nothing. I got assholes who holler out, 'Hey,

Greek, gimme a beer!' and 'Hey, Greek, what's gook cunt like?'
Ever since I got back, it's like I was locked up alone. All alone."

There was quiet awhile longer. The boy, who still moved
slowly and with an occasional hitch in his breath, picked up
another log and shoved it into the stove. He slammed the doors
of the stove shut. It had been the same for them all.

When Billy Leaps spoke again, the tone of his voice was
entirely different. "We have to be in peak shape if we're going
back. It's been eight years. We get older and we get out of shape.
I'm not going back to Indochina with a bunch of guys who
aren't at peak."

"I'm there, man, I'm already there," said Applebaum, punch-
ing his own chest. Rosie grunted disbelief.

"So here's what's up," Billy Leaps continued. "Every day we
begin with exercises. Same as boot camp. I've got it worked out.
Then we go into specialties. Harry, Rosie, the two of you have
got to get back up to marksman status right off. You've been
away from guns for a long time, too long. I've kept up, but of
course it's been easy for me out here in the woods."

Harry and Rosie exchanged glances, and Rosie winked.

"Applebaum, you got to get together the minimal set of
munitions we're going to need. Minimal but complete, you
understand? And don't go overboard. We can't carry around
enough stuff to blow up Cambodia or whatever the hell they call
it now. But you figure out what we need, and put it together. I
imagine you've kept up—"

Applebaum nodded vigorously.

"—so you'll have to catch us up a little."

"It's done," said Applebaum with complacent pride.

"Where you gonna get all this shit?" demanded Rosie skep-
tically.

"I got sources," said Applebaum mysteriously. "I got buddies in every war zone in the world. Every single one. I can get you tanks. I can get you—"

"We don't want tanks," Billy Leaps broke in. "Tanks are not going to be part of this operation."

"But, Beeker," said Harry, "we got to have guns. We got to have Claymores." It was odd how quickly they had fallen into the old roles. After eight long years apart, together again for not more than a few hours, and the Greek was already running interference for Applebaum, just like he used to. "Marty'll do things right."

Rosie suggested something: "If we're supposed to be doing this for the CIA, then why don't we just use Karlsrupas? Hell, they're fine machines. Just fine. And—"

"I want an American gun!" Applebaum shouted.

Everyone ignored him. Billy Leaps replied to the black man, "It'd mean we'd all have to break in on a new weapon—"

"Not me! I know that Kraut gun." There seemed no way to stop Applebaum.

"It's a Swedish weapon, Applebaum." Billy Leaps used the same exaggerated tone of voice he used with his most knuckle-headed students. "Krauts are German, not Swedish."

"Oh."

"Anyway, the Karlsrupa would be a new gun. Yeah, they say that's what the Agency uses. I don't know. I haven't kept up with that. Look, I do know we all used M16s. We'll get those. We don't have time to really learn a new gun. And, anyway, I can get 16s."

"We could break into the Army base, the one right here in Shreveport," suggested Applebaum. His eyes lighted up. "Plenty of M16s there."

"We are not going to start this operation by breaking into a U.S. Army base only thirty miles from my home." Billy Leaps was adamant. "There's a reservist I know, up in Virginia Beach. He can do it. Cowboy, I'm sending you up to Virginia tomorrow morning to pick up the weapons and the ammo. And if somebody finds out, the reservist is the one who'll take the heat. He sells the things as a hunting rifle."

"For blowing away Big Foot," croaked Cowboy, and laughed at his own joke. Nobody else did.

"I want to keep as clean as possible on this," Beeker concluded. "Applebaum, you got that? Clean as possible."

"That means no nukes," said Rosie.

"No nukes," repeated Applebaum carefully, as if getting it straight in his mind.

"Cowboy," said Beeker, "you're the one needs the specialized training least. You've been flying every day. You're going to have to concentrate on your body. It's all shot to hell. That cocaine."

This was the first time that Beeker had ever mentioned Cowboy's mental addiction to the drug.

"Hey, Beeker," he protested, "that stuff keeps me going. Keeps me going and keeps me happy."

"As of right now," said Beeker, "you're off it. Cold turkey. You're in training. We're all in training."

Cowboy sat stunned.

"We're in training," said Billy Leaps, and he spoke to everybody. "That means no liquor; that means no drugs."

The group let out a collective howl.

"What are you talking about, man?" Rosie demanded. "Man, I haven't gone without my dope since I got back, and I'm too old to start doing without it now."

"Beeker, I got to have blow," Cowboy said, regaining his voice. "I mean, I can't open my eyes in the morning without blow."

"No," said Billy Leaps. "We're not boys anymore, not the way we were when we first went over there. When we go back, every one of our faculties will be on top alert. Our bodies will be as good as they were back then. So no drugs. And no liquor.

I'm holding everybody down to two beers a night. Otherwise it won't work. None of it will work unless you do like I say."

"So who are you to tell us no dope, no booze?" Applebaum demanded. He would have. He was the only one who didn't drink hard liquor, and he could take all the drugs in the world and they didn't have any effect on him. Applebaum could shoot up heroin, and then he'd want to go out and play pinball. Nothing Applebaum took into his body made him any more wired or crazy than he already was.

"Beeker's the team leader," said Cowboy, already defending the man he had been ready to kill a few moments ago for taking away his cocaine.

"Says you and who else?" challenged Applebaum.

"Says me," answered Rosie grimly, though not yet resigned to the loss of his half dozen marijuana joints a day.

"And me," said Harry quietly. Up in his two rooms above the bar, Harry had been accustomed to putting away a fifth of Scotch a night.

Applebaum looked round the circle again, meeting every man's eyes. He ended up with Beeker's gaze. "Well, I guess that means you are," he admitted. "I hate that shit anyway."

"We're going to be jungle-ready in two months," said Beeker. "That's why no booze. That's why no blow for Cowboy, and no grass for Rosie."

"Man, we used the junk in *combat*," protested Rosie, though he knew the battle was already lost.

"That's right," said Beeker quickly. "But we were all twenty-three, twenty-four years old. That was ten years ago we were doing that. There's no telling what that stuff would do to us now. Maybe more. Maybe not as much, even. But we're not going to experiment. For now, when we're in training, your asses are mine. And I say two beers a night. Got it?"

"You got it," sighed Rosie. "Utter discipline."

"Awesome discipline," said Cowboy, pale behind his mirrored glasses.

Harry just nodded, then he looked sharply at Applebaum. Applebaum caught his friend's glance and nodded too.

"You want us in shape in two months?" demanded Applebaum. "Hell, I'm in shape now. I never got out of shape." He sprang to his feet. He threw his eyeglasses onto the table. "You just look and see." He dropped quickly to the floor, barely catching himself on his outstretched palms. "One. Two. Three. Four . . ." He counted off push-ups.

The others ignored him and went over into the corner to divvy up sleeping bags and blankets for the night.

". . . Seventeen. Eighteen. Nineteen."

Applebaum suddenly noticed that he didn't have an audience. He hopped to his feet again.

Cowboy turned and tossed a sleeping bag at him. "Here," he said. "Outside."

"What the hell do you mean, Cowboy?"

"You are not fit to sleep inside with the rest of us, Applebaum," said Cowboy. "I know you. I knew you for too many years. And you haven't changed, except your skin's cleared up. As soon as you get your hands on one of those nice M16s, you're going to start taking it to bed with you every night. You're going to play out being a SEALs asshole and wrap your arms around it. Then you're going to have one of your fucking nightmares one night and start shooting up the house. I'm not putting up with it. So that's what I mean when I say 'Outside.'"

"Outside," Rosie agreed. "I remember your strange shit in the middle of the night. You don't belong in here with us civilized persons."

"What about Harry? Huh? What about Harry? Harry has

nightmares too. Worse than mine. Huh? You gonna put up with Harry's crying and screaming? He does that every night. Not just once in a while. Isn't that right, Harry?" Harry said nothing, but he looked embarrassed. Yet strangely, he wasn't embarrassed for himself, for the weakness inside his head that brought the nightmares on every night, but embarrassed for Applebaum's sake, that Applebaum should treat him like that in front of the team. "You gonna let Harry stay?" Applebaum concluded bitterly.

"Harry stays," said Beeker. "You go out. You're an animal, right? So you go out." That ended the conversation.

Applebaum kicked the floor in frustration, but he had to give in. What did it matter where he slept so long as the team was together again? He went outside and slammed the door shut behind him. By the time he had arranged his bag under a tree and had crawled inside it, he could see the lights in the cabin being extinguished, one by one.

9

Billy Leaps woke Rosie up the next morning, cautioning him to be quiet and not disturb the others. He motioned the black man to dress and follow him.

In a couple of minutes they were outside, walking toward Beeker's truck. The Louisiana dawn was frosty. Their breath congealed. "Where we going?" whispered Rosie, his throat rasping with sleep.

"Got to go to the school I worked at, the academy."

"What for?" Rosie challenged, though he obediently climbed into the passenger seat of the pickup. He waited for his answer until Beeker had the engine started and had pulled out onto the driveway.

"We need some equipment. We need some food too. The food I'll buy. The equipment the academy owes me."

"You're the boss," said Rosie, shrugging. He leaned his head against the back of the seat and fitfully resumed his night's rest while the truck bounced over the county back roads.

When the truck came to a halt, Rosie opened his eyes quickly. He looked around at the school's impressive physical plant. It looked like a place that would be called Shreveport Academy for Young Men. "You worked *here*, Beeker?"

"Ignore the outside. All fake. Rotten on the inside." His words were bitter.

Billy Leaps had parked the truck on the grass right beside the back entrance of the brick gymnasium. He still had keys, a duplicate set that he had retained after his firing. He led Rosie to the equipment room. The men struggled to take out sets of weights, workout clothes, basketballs, and soccer balls.

"These?" Rosie whispered, but whispering was unnecessary, for there was no one else in the building at six a.m.

"Good for the coordination" was all that Billy Leaps would say.

They got most everything to the truck in three quick trips. Billy Leaps led a wondering Rosie back inside. He pointed to a large Universal machine in a corner and tossed Rosie a wrench. They dismantled it quickly and carried it out to the truck.

Beeker locked the doors again, pocketed the keys, and then climbed into the truck. He started the engine and drove quietly off the school property. Not far away the headmaster and the boarding boys were still sleeping in the master's house and dormitories.

"They're going to miss this stuff," said Rosie, with a slight tone of warning in his voice.

"They owe it to me, like I said."

"Aren't they going to figure out who took it?"

"Sure," said Billy Leaps with a grim smile, "but they know I could sue their pants off for firing me the way they did. I don't care what kind of fake evidence Parkes cooked up. Firing a Native American without cause still doesn't look good when it's brought up before the Civil Rights Commission."

Rosie nodded. He found himself juggling a half dozen game

balls in the cab of the truck as Billy Leaps drove it down the highway. "Basketball and soccer? Beeker, I'm thirty-seven years old."

"And you look it. But in two months you won't." It was the end of the conversation so far as Billy Leaps was concerned.

In the Piggly Wiggly they bought dozens of eggs, several pounds of bacon, gallons of orange juice and milk. He loaded the basket with whole wheat bread, a couple of sides of ham, and an enormous roast beef. He added a twenty-five-pound bag of potatoes—from the same farm where he had dug potatoes as a teenager—and an armful of various green vegetables.

"No ice cream?"

Beeker looked at Rosie in disbelief, then realized he was serious. "No ice cream."

"Even the fucking Army gave us ice cream!"

"That's why the fucking Army is like it is," said Billy Leaps. "It serves too much goddamn ice cream."

It was strange that even after so long the internecine rivalry remained. It had been considered Billy Leaps's greatest accomplishment that he had managed to put together a team composed of two Army men, two Navy men, and himself, their Marine leader. It was a wonder they had survived Vietnam, and it was a wonder they hadn't all killed one another.

When they drove into the farmyard, only the boy was visible. He ran up and followed Billy Leaps's directions on unloading the food. Leaving the boy to the job—he obviously didn't want any help in this—Billy Leaps went over to where Applebaum still slept.

"Hey, Beeker," Rosie said, laughing, "remember what they say about waking up a SEAL. You gotta tickle their feet and run like hell. Only way to do it without getting yourself killed."

Rosie stopped laughing when he realized that Beeker intended to do almost that. Billy Leaps had leaned over Applebaum, yelled, and grabbed a foot through the cover of the sleeping bag. Then the Cherokee stepped quickly back. Apple-baum rose up in a rush and tripped himself over the cloth that contained him. He pitched forward onto the still frosty grass. "Bastard! Bastard!" the little blond man yelled insanely, struggling to stand up, trying to get out of the zipper bag, and attempting to strike out at Billy Leaps all at once. "Bastard, you bastard."

"Better than an alarm clock," said Billy Leaps to Rosie with a grin. He turned toward the house. Applebaum's screams had wakened Harry and Cowboy. They rushed outside in their underwear and looked around quickly to see what the hell was going on.

"Come on," said Billy Leaps, "time to start."

Applebaum's face was red with frustration. Beeker ignored him and spoke to the whole group. "Look around at yourselves. You're all out of shape. But we're going to start easy, just some exercises in the morning, a quick run. Then breakfast and a short break. You can use the break to read up on your specialties and get to know your M16s better."

They all muttered curses at this regimen. Every man remembered the endlessly repetitive breaking down and putting together of their arms. They had hated to do it in Vietnam, and they'd hate to do it now. But they knew they had to. Whatever else they fucked up in Asia, they had never fucked up cleaning and loving their weapons. They all knew they wouldn't be alive today if they had.

"Then, some work on the weights. We'll break for a little game then—just fun, soccer, maybe basketball. A little lunch, light, so you don't have too much to digest. Then Rosie, Harry, and me will do some shooting. We can start on my hunting rifles until the M16s get here tomorrow."

"Tomorrow?" Cowboy broke in.

Beeker nodded. "No reason for you not to fly up today, pick up the stuff, and fly back first thing in the morning. No reason at all."

"But to be that close to D.C.! Come on, Beeker, I'll be that close to D.C. and I got a lady there . . ."

"We need the arms tomorrow, first thing. And you need the exercise, now and tomorrow both." Beeker's tone of voice didn't allow argument. "Then we'll run again before dinner. Some more reading, and that'll be it."

The men stood silently for a moment. Then Harry turned to Rosie. "I sure do hope he gives us five minutes in there somewhere for those two beers."

"I hope I have the energy to lift the bottle," Rosie returned. "You know how Beeker is when he says 'A little run. A few exercises.'"

Harry groaned and patted his belly. "Yeah, I know."

"Get some stuff from the pile now," said Beeker. "It's just running stuff: shoes and shorts, jocks, shirts if you want them. We'll work our way up to packs in a couple of days."

"Packs?" Cowboy cried. "In a couple of days?"

"We're going back" was all Beeker said.

The following evening Cowboy headed his plane toward the landing strip at Beeker's farm. It had been a long and exhausting round trip. He had made it just a little bit longer by circling around Birmingham three times to see if he couldn't keep himself from that last run before dinner. Jesus Christ, his body was screaming in agony over the first morning's trials. Just a little run, just a little game, and goddamn, but wasn't Billy Leaps a sweetheart, letting him get in the goddamn Universal machine for an hour before he took off for Virginia.

Everything ached. Everything. His arms were stiff, his legs

were tight with agony, his stomach growled with displeasure at the strained muscles that kept it in. He felt muscles just behind his rib cage that he had forgotten about for eight years, and right now they were singing out to be noticed. *Here we are, here we are, Cowboy remember us?* If Billy Leaps could do this to him in one morning, what the hell was Cowboy in for over the next two months, he wondered. And Mother C banished from the door!

Cowboy let his airspeed down a little more as he crossed the Mississippi. He'd get in just before dark. What the hell—so long as he made it back with the weapons, right? He had really thought that it would be impossible for Billy Leaps to arrange for the whole pickup and delivery in time for him to return in one overnight trip anyway. But those fucking jarheads stayed together.

Beeker'd just called his Marine buddy who operated a "hunting gun" store out of his basement in Virginia Beach. Then there was a drill instructor who knew a couple of guys who'd have use of a truck and would take a day off for a single note each. And another reservist who could make sure that the local cops weren't paying too much attention at the airport that night. And all Cowboy had to show up with was four thousand dollars in cash and greetings from Billy Leaps Beeker. And goddamn them all if they hadn't pulled it off as though they were going to invade Libya all by themselves. Fucking jarheads never got to be civilians. And now they had worked together to deprive him of a single night in D.C. on a two-thousand-mile trip back and forth from Shreveport. One night of exhausted sleep in a cheap holiday motel, and there they were—all the bastards spilled out of the same mold as Billy Leaps—knocking at his door and waking him up at break of dawn, the fucking plane already loaded, clearance to take off all set, fuel all taken care of, and "Move your ass. Beeker's waiting."

Hell, if he *had* headed the plane up to D.C., he probably would have been intercepted by a Phantom or some shit like that. Goddamn the Marines to hell.

As the plane lost altitude, Cowboy thought something looked strange below. The configuration of Beeker's fields was different somehow, subtly altered from when he'd taken off the day before. He was wary as he made his landing, though that was as smooth as ever.

They were all there waiting for him when he climbed out of the plane. "You got it?" Beeker asked.

"Great to see you again too," Cowboy answered. He looked at them. They had just returned from their "little run," and sweat poured from their brows. Rosie and Harry were sitting on the ground, and it looked as if only pride kept them from stretching out at full length on the dead autumn grass. Cowboy knew that Applebaum wanted to throw himself down beside them but was too tough to admit it. As if anybody cared what the fucker felt like inside. Anyway, Applebaum had claimed he was in shape. Maybe he had been. To anybody's standards but Beeker's. Billy Leaps's shirt was just as soaked as the others', but he certainly looked as if he were holding up better.

"Okay, let's get this stuff unloaded." Billy Leaps slapped his hands together.

"Oh, come on, Beeker, after dinner, after dinner." Harry's voice was weak and winded.

"Let's go."

They moved slowly toward the plane. "You," Beeker said to Cowboy, "you can get another hour on that machine before dinner. Get rid of your pilot seat cramps."

"Hey, Billy Leaps, it's me! Cowboy! I just flew in from Virginia, remember? And you want me . . ."

The other men were moving toward Cowboy now. A sudden

emotion flared in their eyes. Rosie's voice was ominous. "You get those clothes off and you get in your jockstrap and you start working that iron. Like the rest of us did all day while you were up in the clouds. If you think you're going to pussyface your way around this camp after what we've been through today, you are full of shit."

"Hey, guys, Virginia. Virginia . . ."

Harry's voice was nearly as menacing as Rosie's. "You get on that fucking machine before I wrap it around your fucking neck."

"Okay, guys, okay." Cowboy wasn't stupid. He knew when to give in. "I'm going. Right now. I'm going right now and work out."

"Just an hour," said Billy Leaps, as if he were making some special concession. "And concentrate on where it already hurts most. But just an hour."

"Oh, gee thanks, Beeker, thanks a lot." The sarcasm in Cowboy's voice wilted when the men started to turn on him again. "I'm going, I'm going."

Cowboy was the last to take his shower. He came into the main room still rubbing his hair with his towel. "Thanks a lot, guys, for leaving me all that hot water. I just about scalded my nuts off in there."

"There's no hot water," said Billy Leaps. He was dishing mounds of mashed potatoes onto a platter.

Cowboy was puzzled. He'd used that shower often. "Heater broke?"

"Nope." Billy Leaps scooped more potatoes out of the pan. "Turned it off."

"Off!" Cowboy's cry was matched with slight groans from Rosie and Harry, who had thought that Applebaum had used up all the warm water.

"For the next two months."

Cowboy collapsed onto a chair at the table in defeat. This time he didn't even try to argue with Beeker.

They ate voraciously, and in silence. When he had finished his second helping of everything, Cowboy turned to Beeker and asked, "Something was different down here. Something about the farm. I could tell from the air. What'd you do?"

Harry broke into a loud guffaw. Rosie grimaced. Applebaum grinned broadly.

Billy Leaps smiled as he answered: "Well, seeing as how Applebaum's gotta have something to practice with, I figured he might as well do some good, you know? So I gave him what dynamite I had and started him clearing off some of the scrub oak."

"All afternoon, man," complained Rosie. "Boom, BOOM, *BOOM!*"

"Yeah!" cried Applebaum, with uninfectious enthusiasm. "Might as well get an extra acre or two out of this," said Billy Leaps.

"And we get to move the dead wood while we wait for our turn on the machine," said Harry. "You missed that part today. You'll pick it up tomorrow."

"Before the soccer game," said Rosie.

"Which is before the evening run," said Applebaum.

"Oh, shit," Cowboy said.

It was going to be hell.

10

They were ready in seven weeks.

It had been hell.

But they were ready. Their bodies had shed flab but gained pounds—pounds of muscle. All five had spent entire days driving themselves. Sleep was the only brief respite from the torture.

They had all had the raw material. They were out of shape, sure, but their bodies remembered. Even Cowboy hadn't lost everything. And their minds remembered, too.

First they had remembered the pain of it all. The excruciating pain of working your muscles to the maximum. Billy Leaps had learned all about muscles. He knew to rotate his men's exercises and to change their routines so they were doing the most good in the shortest span of time. He knew how to feed them. Their diet was high-protein and well balanced. Their appetites were boundless. Their capacity for milk and meat had become awesome within the first week. Their bodies craved protein the way Cowboy's mind had craved cocaine.

Their desire for alcohol and drugs had dissipated into the night air.

At first it had been a survival instinct. They had all gone through one boot camp for their service and then had returned for a much tougher tenure for special training. Rosie hadn't thought much of plain old Army boot camp, but Green Beret training had showed him what the Army could do when it put its scattered mind to the task. Applebaum had had to prove himself at the SEALs training center—Great Lake was too easy. Same for Harry. So they remembered what they had had to do to survive those double tortures. They were all going through it again, a third time.

Sleep as soon as you could. Get every single minute that was possible. Eat what was put in front of you and down it immediately before it could be taken away from you. And time yourself, pace yourself, but don't let anybody think you're trying to get away with anything easy. They'll just double the work. Just get through it like a man, at a man's pace. Don't play pussyface slacker, and don't show off either. Even Applebaum got roped down to the routine.

At night they were exhausted. The food and the lessons and the crackling fire drove all of them to bed as soon as Beeker allowed them. They woke at the crack of dawn, not from any call or signal, but merely from the knowledge that this was something that had to be done.

They were going to be at war. The mission itself seemed to slip from their minds. They rarely thought of Gougelmann and his seventeen compatriots in the Laotian prison camp. That hardly seemed to matter anymore. They only knew that they were a team, and that the team was going into battle again. This knowledge flooded their subconscious. It dictated their actions and their feelings and their very cravings. They didn't want the dope. They didn't even want the beer. They wanted the alertness back. Once they had found their peak, then they could fuck with it. Let one another turn on, one by one, maybe. But they had to get to peak first.

The growing awareness of their bodies brought back their

memories. The fire fights, the explosions. Even Applebaum seemed to grow sober. He wasn't showing off anymore when he went into the woods and practiced his technique with plastiques and grenades and Claymores. It came back to him how devastating it could be—would be—if his aim was off, if his timing was fractured, if his wiring was sloppy. They could die. All of them could die because of him.

And Marty had to learn to make love to his M60 again. He had screamed and yelled at Beeker. "Can't make me go into battle without my M60." The others were comfortable with their automatic rifles, but Applebaum had to have his goddamn machine gun.

Beeker gave in. Another phone call to Virginia Beach, and the next day an air freight delivery service arrived with the crate. Applebaum opened it up and assembled the machinery with Christmas morning glee. To Rosie's disgust he had taken the boy out into the woods to show him the awesome ability of the M60. He had used the weapon with its immense firepower to cut down a forty-year oak with one volley. The boy had been impressed, no doubt about it. Anyone would be impressed with an M60.

But as the days went on, Applebaum began to see it differently, probably because no one ragged him about it. He realized that he'd be the one carrying it into the field. He and this piece of equipment might save all the others. He stopped showing off for the boy. He no longer bragged about his new piece of weaponry. Instead, he practiced soberly and treated the gun with respect. Because he knew that he and that M60 might be all that stood between the Black Berets and death.

The same realization played in Harry's mind as he worked on the makeshift target range with Billy Leaps and Rosie. If he didn't shoot the target just right the first time with the single shot—they could die.

But Harry had an additional assignment. His M16 was

different from the others'. His had an M203 attached below the barrel, just a little piece of metal that altered his rifle from a deadly personal weapon to a frightening grenade launcher. He had enough extra ammunition—special ammunition—to make Applebaum jealous. It hung from a special belt. There were fléchette rounds, like great shredding shotgun shells; gas rounds that could burn out a man's lungs if bullets or shrapnel couldn't find his flesh; high explosive rounds that would burst armor—or blow a building; and willy peter—white phosphorus rounds to torch a position or erase the darkness that the enemy used as a weapon.

Harry practiced. He knew his weapon. He knew his ammo. Just in case he had to save all their lives with one of them. Because if Harry didn't do it right that first time, if he didn't know just what to use and where to find it, if he didn't get his rounds off fast enough—they just might all die.

There was no room for error. None. Harry had to be right on target. So did Rosie. And Rosie was onto something else. He thought at first it was bullshit to read all his books again, the books that taught the medic how to play god-doctor in the field. But if he didn't remember just how to tie that tourniquet and how to close that wound, then one of these men might die. Because of him.

There was a progression to it all, a growing awareness not of what they had to do, but of what they had to be. They were quieter around one another now. And it wasn't just that they were too tired to talk. Each man was newly infused with the awareness that he was going to trust his life to the other four, that his survival depended as much on them as upon himself. Each man knew that he was responsible not only for the success of his part of the mission, but of the lives of his four friends. It was just like Nam. Just like Cambodia. Just like . . .

It was what none of the men had felt since returning to the States.

All their perceptions changed. The process was slow, sometimes so slow they wouldn't realize that anything had happened till afterward. Things like: Cowboy suddenly didn't think it was so funny that Applebaum did indeed sleep with his new M60. It had seemed like such an asshole thing to do, sleep with a gun. But one night, just as he was falling asleep, something nagged at Cowboy. It was his own M16. It was over with the rest of them, carefully stacked up against the wall. It didn't seem right to him that it was so far away, all the way across the room. Hell, he was only in Louisiana on a godforsaken farm in a godforsaken corner of a county nobody had ever heard of—but you just couldn't be too careful. So he went and got the M16 and carefully rested it closer to him, within quick reach. That night, despite the cold, he slept with his arms outside the sleeping bag, just in case he had to get at the weapon quickly.

The next morning when Cowboy saw Applebaum's M60 up and ready alongside his sleeping bag under the oak, Applebaum just didn't seem to be quite so much of an asshole anymore. Cowboy even realized that Applebaum had stopped complaining about being forced to sleep outside. He seemed to take pride in his compatriots' picture of him as an uncivilized animal. And even that tattoo on Applebaum's arm didn't seem so stupid anymore, not when the muscles under it were like rope.

The kid didn't understand all that was going on. He joined in, as much as his recovering wounds would allow, playing basketball and soccer with the five men. He ran in the morning and the evening, and in the afternoon he worked out whenever the Universal machine was free. The men were good to him. He didn't know why. But he was as glad of it as he was frightened that it would end abruptly.

For foster kids, happiness was always short-lived, and the

ending was always abrupt. It was a car ride away from the scene of the brief happiness. That's all. You just got in a welfare worker's car and were driven away, never to return.

Sometimes the men looked funny at him. Especially Rosie. The boy didn't know why, and he didn't ask. That was his way. He didn't know that Rosie was remembering. Remembering other kids.

There had been one in camp. A kid even younger than this one. Eight, nine years old maybe. An orphan, anxious for food, and willing to do anything the GI Joes wanted him to do. The GI Joes had gotten lazy in this forgotten corner of the war. Even the Green Berets had grown slack in that particular sector. They trusted people; they had wanted to believe all the government bullshit about saving the "indigenous population" from the Cong, from the Communist North.

So there was this kid. Cute as could be. Rosie gave him chocolate bars all the time. The kid would run errands, he'd dig latrines, hell, he got to the point where he could clean a rifle as well as just about anybody but Rosie himself.

Then one day a cracker from South Carolina that Rosie never liked walked away from camp with the kid. The kid was laughing and carrying on, and then suddenly he started to run. He ran like hell, all the laughter gone from his face. Rosie and the other guys, the survival instinct hard upon them, fell into foxholes. Not the cracker. He called after the kid. He was still calling the kid when the grenade exploded, the grenade the kid had dropped between the cracker's legs. The legs that weren't attached to his body anymore.

They had gone after the kid, cursing themselves for their trust. If he had been a thirteen-year-old, they wouldn't have had anything to do with him. It was easy to imagine a thirteen-year-old infiltrator. Hell, those guys they were sending down along the Ho Chi Minh Trail were thirteen and fourteen. But an eight-year-old? What the hell did an eight-year-old know about politics? Or hand grenades? They found the kid. And this sergeant, the kindest man Rosie had ever met in the U.S. Army, had been sobbing when he took out his pistol and put it to the head of the eight-year-old Vietnamese youngster. The boy spat in the sergeant's face less than a second before the sergeant pulled the trigger.

When you've seen an eight-year-old kill a grown man with a grenade, cracker or no, then you realize that the enemy could be anybody at all. When you have to watch a sergeant who was the nicest man in the world kill the little bastard with a bullet to the forehead, well then, you just don't look at kids the same anymore. Not when you're training for war.

But Beeker's kid was careful. He was cautious for lots of reasons. He wasn't going to do anything to jeopardize staying on with Billy Leaps. So he never intruded himself. He saw that some things were taken too seriously for him to be a part of. He desperately wanted Billy Leaps to show him how to shoot a gun as well as the others did. But when Beeker, Rosie, and Harry went out toward the range together, they looked so intent that the boy never followed. When certain looks came over Rosie's face, the kid made himself scarce. He stayed out of Applebaum's way all the time. He wasn't going to challenge them.

He made himself as useful as he could be. He knew a little about cooking, so he saw to it that there were always enough potatoes peeled and ready to cook when the men came in for dinner. The wood stove was stoked when it needed to be. He didn't yet know anything about farming, but it was still winter, and little needed to be done on that score. Billy Leaps had his own washing machine in a corner of the kitchen, and the boy figured out how to use it. He did endless loads of washing and hung it out to dry. In short, the kid made things go right.

He was pleased when he got any sort of thanks for his efforts. He was more pleased when they were taken for granted. He wanted the five men to assume that he belonged there. He had never before belonged anywhere. It was as if he had spent his whole life at a series of bus stops, always waiting for the next vehicle to come along and take him to the next bus stop. But finally he felt he had reached a destination. This was where he wanted to be. These were men he wanted to know. He wanted to earn their respect. He wanted to be, in some small way, a part of their team.

So, at the end of seven weeks they were ready. They were at peak, and they felt it, individually and as a team. "Beeker, I want to *do* something," Rosie said suddenly one night.

"Yeah," agreed Harry and Cowboy.

"No more school shit," Applebaum said. And for once no one disagreed with him.

Billy Leaps didn't hesitate. He had evidently been thinking about this too. "We're going camping. South of here, near Lake Charles. There's some wild places, bayous and the like. We'll do survival camping. Rations. Forced marches. We'll test ourselves against real stuff for a change."

Everyone agreed, and Rosie wanted to start the next day.

"Three days," said Billy Leaps. "I got to get things ready."

"Like what?" demanded Cowboy.

"Like packs," said the Cherokee. "Like uniforms."

"What about our old cammies?" asked Rosie.

"Only Applebaum and me got the whole set," replied Beeker.

"We can get stuff at a surplus store," Harry suggested.

"Not good enough," Beeker replied.

"What the hell you want, you fucking jarhead?" Cowboy demanded. They had all become more short and aggressive in their dealings with one another. "You want us to go into the bayous wearing Marine dress blues?"

"I want us to wear what we're going to be wearing over there."

"The man wants three days, give him three days," said Harry.

The next morning Billy Leaps drove into town with the boy, and an hour later returned with an old Indian woman hunched down in the cab between them. Both Billy Leaps and the boy showed her great respect. Beeker called the men together. "Line up," he said.

The old Cherokee woman was a seamstress.

Quickly and expertly, never saying a word and never looking up into any of the men's eyes, the old woman whipped her measuring tape across their bodies, up the inside and outside of their legs, around their thighs. She carried a worn little notebook in one hand and marked down a whole line of figures.

She finished quickly and said something to Billy Leaps. She spoke in Cherokee, and no one understood her but Billy Leaps and the boy. They glanced at one another. Billy Leaps answered the old woman's question: "Measure the boy too."

11

They waked a little later the following Friday morning. Billy Leaps had declared a kind of semiholiday for the trip south. Their packs had been put together the night before, and their guns cleaned the last thing before bed. After breakfast each of the men said good-bye to the boy and went to the truck.

The four of them climbed into the back of the truck and arranged themselves as comfortably as possible on the gritty metal bed. None of them was going to ride in the cab with Billy Leaps. They all seemed to know that. The Cherokee drove the truck out the now familiar road and eventually onto the Interstate heading south.

The four of them rode silently, thinking of the ordeal ahead. It was always worse than you imagined, and their imagination about such things was pretty well developed. They wore street clothes because Beeker didn't want any attention drawn to them. All their gear was hidden, in the cab of the truck and under blankets in the back. But passing motorists still stared at the sight of four grown men riding in the bed of a pickup truck on the Interstate. They might have looked like convicts, but they hadn't any prison garb and weren't chained together.

"You wouldn't laugh at us if we had our uniforms on right now, you bet your ass you wouldn't laugh," Harry said aloud, but the noise of the truck and the wind covered his words.

At first Harry and the others had been skeptical about the necessity of having the old Cherokee woman sew them uniforms from scratch, from bolts of cloth that Billy Leaps had chosen himself. They all knew that Billy Leaps cared about uniforms as only a Marine could. Even as SEALs, Applebaum and Harry himself didn't come close. But the uniform—whatever form it took—meant something to Billy Leaps. He got into it. And his quiet enthusiasm had become infectious.

As Harry and the others handled the new clothes that Billy Leaps fetched from the old Cherokee woman's home, a strangeness came over them, just like the slow strangeness that had come over them in the course of their training. Magic resided in a man's uniform. Something magic, and yet something very, very real.

The black canvaslike material had been stiff in Harry's hands. He had had clothing like this before. It would change after it had been washed. It would become looser. It would give more. It would move as his body moved, without resistance. He had wanted to put it on immediately and was disappointed to hear Billy Leaps tell the boy to gather all the new clothes together and wash them. Harry was the last to give his up.

Billy Leaps pulled onto a dirt road. He drove down it for a few miles, then turned off into the forest on a disused logging track. It was early afternoon. They had killed some time with lunch at a diner. They had eaten the meal slowly and had given it much more respect than a highway grease joint deserved. They didn't know how long it would be before they had another real meal.

Billy Leaps had even refused to tell them how long this venture would last.

"A man who marks time is a fuck-up," said Billy Leaps, and nobody asked again.

The truck bumped along for another couple of miles, the ground becoming softer and spongier. When Beeker halted, the men climbed down off the truck bed, bringing their packs and other stores with them. Billy Leaps stood in front of the group. "So far as I'm concerned, this is for real. This is the real thing. So after we've hidden the truck, we're going to dress up. And after we've dressed up, we're going in there." He jerked his head toward the thick underbrush of the Louisiana bayou country. "We're going in there, and we're going to act like it's Nam."

Billy Leaps drove the truck off the logging track into a thick straggling stand of underbrush. In a moment the truck was nearly invisible. The vegetation was so thick around the cab of the truck that the Indian had to climb out of the window and swing onto the truck bed. In ten minutes the five men had succeeded in disguising the truck so effectively, that no one would have found it who didn't actually stumble into that one particular tangled stand of underbrush and scrub wood. This wasn't a necessary precaution, for in the Louisiana backwoods a man's truck was safe even if he went away for a month and didn't even bother to take out the keys. Still, the exercise put the men into the right frame of mind.

With the truck now invisible even to them, they were alone in the Louisiana bayous.

Harry dug out the uniform. He laid it out on the ground with solemnity. The pants were spread out, over them the shirt. The socks were neatly stacked beside them. The boots. The beret. The belt. The small pack of essentials. The larger pack. The knives. The guns. He stood back and surveyed the familiar gear. There was a blueprint in his mind: a place for everything, everything in its place.

He was oblivious to the other men as he stripped naked. He didn't need to be. For these few minutes all five members of the team were solitary individuals. Alone with their uniforms, they were remembering. As each man picked up the first article of clothing, he was hurtled back.

Harry pulled on the pants. No underwear to bind or give him crotch rot. The pants were loose so as not to restrict movement. In no place would those pants ever bind him. The baggy legs would be caught tightly by the boots. He took the webbed belt with its buckle painted over with dull black enamel. All black. If the enemy didn't have a target to fire at, they couldn't get you. Harry drew in his breath. How long he'd lived in clothes like these!

He pulled on the shirt. Like the pants, he was wearing the camouflage side out. The old Cherokee woman had sewn the clothes in such a way that one side was like this, wandering stripes of greens, olives, and black. The clothes were reversible. On the back was just black cloth, for night, for darkness. Harry dragged on the heavy socks, designed to absorb shock when he ran, to cushion his feet mile after wearying mile. Then he stepped into the boots. The familiar jungle boots. The canvas/leather/plastic boots had been regulation in Vietnam after many false starts. Too often American combat troops tried to go into battle with footwear that couldn't survive the rigors of the jungle. Billy Leaps had found them at a surplus store. Eight years after the U.S. had left Indochina, and the fucking Army was probably still requisitioning them. Harry knelt down first on one knee and then on the other to lace them up. Their tight grip on his ankles was something he hadn't forgotten after all these years. It was part of him, and that part came back in a wave of painful nostalgia. Those fucking boots!

Finally, he picked up the beret that Billy Leaps had handed him, handed all of them as they stepped into the muck. He put it on his head and had a sudden urge to cry, to have tears wash down his face and take away the memory of what it had meant to wear an outfit like this. He knew what was going to happen to it—exactly what had happened in Nam. They'd go through the bayous wearing these clothes, sleeping in them, marching in them, with never an opportunity to take them off, much less wash them. Over the days the cloth was going to absorb his smell. The uniform would turn into a stink of his flesh and his sweat. It would crust for a bit at first, then the bodily fluids would revive it. Soon he would be able to tell who was near him simply by the odor, as distinctive to a man as his fingerprints or his voice or his walk.

This uniform was going to be like a second skin. Just the way it had been in Nam. He hated these clothes. He hated them because they reminded him of the smell of napalm and the screams of men and women and children who were dying without cause and without remedy. He hated the clothes because they forced him to a peak higher than the one they had all risen to in their training. He felt alert, aware and conscious of every-thing around him. The sounds made by the other men became suddenly and acutely clear to him. He knew what each of them was doing by a whisper of cloth or the click of a fingernail against metal. He heard some small animal breaking through the brush. It was curious at first, then he could sense its fear. Harry picked up his gun and cradled it in his arms.

He was a warrior again. He was returning to combat. He hated these clothes because that's what they did to him. The simple act of putting them on did that to him. He was always so close to the edge anyway, and just the smell of those jungle boots, just the click of the enameled belt buckle, could push him over the edge. He loved this uniform, loved it because it made him a whole man again.

He looked at the others. They were all dressed. Exactly the way he was dressed. They were in uniform, and they were a team. They were the men who had found something in themselves in Nam that few others did. They had found their destiny as warriors, their private tribe of five. Even the squabbling that had been endemic among the various military groups in Vietnam—the Green Berets despising the SEALs who hated the Marines—had been overcome by these five men's recognition of the essential warrior mentality in one another. They had been the one team that could always do the job, that never cracked, that always returned whole. They had seen it all in Nam, and when they got back, they never tried to deny what had happened to them. They had not been ashamed of the regret they felt that it was all over.

After Nam it had seemed that nothing could touch them. Nothing could get through. They were men still, but the Warrior—their essential identity—had been left behind, in a wallow of corruption and misplanning and snaring hypocrisy.

But now they were together again. It was frightening. Exhilarating. It was madness. It was the first moment of sanity that Harry had experienced in years.

In virtual silence things happened now that made perfect sense to Harry, though at the same time he had an almost overpowering sense of their strangeness. Over to one side Rosie had knelt down, his head bared. Billy Leaps stood over him with a canister of shaving cream and a cutthroat razor. He smeared the top of the black man's massive head. Rosie had always had his head shaved before combat. And Billy Leaps had said this was real. Therefore Rosie knelt and presented his head for the razor. The period between then and now collapsed into nothing. It was nothing. They were going back.

Harry went over to Applebaum. They knew what was next. They knelt facing one another. Applebaum handed Harry the cammy paint. Harry closed his eyes for the briefest moment, then accepted the offering. He opened the containers. He dug his fingers into the grease. Then he began to smear it over Applebaum's pale, white face.

The long thick stripes of green went on first. Then the olive. Then the darker olive. They didn't speak a word. You couldn't count on finding a mirror in the Indochinese jungle, but you always had a buddy. Harry and Applebaum had done this for each other hundreds of times over there. They had been together longer than any of the others. They had gone through SEALs training; they had survived years of combat together even before Billy Leaps had found and recruited them. They knew about each other. Applebaum knew about . . . he knew things about Harry.

When Harry was done, Applebaum began to paint the Greek's face in the same patterns. Harry wasn't used to the touch of a man. This was just about the only time he felt it, this and a haircut at the barber's. The roughness of Applebaum's calloused hands and the sharpness of his movements were for a few moments unfamiliar. Then Harry began to remember that touch as well. Time collapsed. Everything that had existed in that bar in Chicago began to evaporate. To boil away into insubstantial steam.

Applebaum finally wiped his hands on the grass. It was always a tough job to do Harry, his beard was so harsh and stubbly. In another couple of days Harry would be wearing a natural camouflage mask of wiry black hair almost up to his eyes. Applebaum and Harry stood up and looked at each other for a long time. Or it seemed like a long time. Harry thought about the sight of a man's face in camouflage. How strange. How familiar.

Cowboy and Rosie were doing the same reciprocal painting job now. The two of them were moving in the same ways Harry and Applebaum had. They were creating new images for each other, taking each other back through time, back across a false destiny to their true one. They were making themselves warriors.

They finished quickly. Rosie's head glistened from the fresh shaving. Harry thought about the touch of the razor on the skull. He wondered about having his own head shorn. But no, that was Rosie's. Besides, Harry didn't need any more symbols.

He got one more, though. He watched as Cowboy and Rosie stood up, their hands still stained with cammy grease. Billy Leaps stood watching them. He had crossed his arms over his chest, unconsciously assuming the traditional Indian stance. Cowboy and Rosie approached him. He didn't move. They each took fingers of grease from the paint cans and began to streak his face, each taking one side.

Watching, Harry felt more than the few years between now and Vietnam slip away. It seemed as if whole centuries were being erased. He had seldom before thought of Beeker as an Indian, but right now he would have sworn that he was watching some distant ancestor of Billy Leaps Beeker being adorned with the war paint of the Cherokee.

The five of them were a tribe. They were warriors. Beeker was their leader. He was their chief.

Rosie finished and drew away.

With two fingers of black grease, Cowboy unflinchingly painted Billy Leaps's mangled ear.

12

They tramped through the bayous. Billy Leaps had done this often. He had the map, but he didn't need it. This was a pastime of his, to come down here and hunt and camp. There were trails, and that was too bad, because there probably wouldn't be trails where they were going. He searched out the densest most overgrown areas, and he led his men through.

He didn't worry about them. They had trained hard and well. At some point you stopped worrying about your men, and you assumed they were following you.

They slogged through marshes. Billy Leaps led them across one small river where the neck-high water forced them to carry their packs and weapons high above their heads on outstretched arms. He knew a ford farther up the river, but this had to be real. In Laos Billy Leaps might not know where a ford was. Their practice would be worthless unless it tested them to the utmost.

They ran faster when they got to the other side. He gave them no time to drain their shoes. Their clothes were heavy with the water. Their feet were soaked with the river silt that had been trapped by the soles of their boots and by their socks. They ran for a full mile before he let them slow down.

The sun was hot above the canopy of cypress and oak. It made the bayou water in their clothes stink. Their sweat merged with it, and the stench was different from what it had been in Nam, but it was just as pungent. And it was only going to get worse.

They pitched camp at sundown. No campfire was allowed. They were in the field, and they were in enemy territory. That meant no fire, ever, not even a cigarette. That meant keeping their weapons at ready at all times. That meant never getting out of camouflage and paint.

Billy Leaps roused his men at midnight. Though they had not expected to be summoned, they were instantly awake. Billy Leaps opened a map of the area on the ground, and by the dim light of the waning moon, he showed them where they were and where the nearest campgrounds were. He sent the men off in pairs, with instructions for the pairs to break up a little farther on. Their first mission was to bring back some small unimportant item from the middle of a campground. It was a simple test of stealth.

After his men took off, Billy Leaps went too. He was confident he'd have the easiest time because he was used to the area. It took him an hour to find his destination, the smallest of the campgrounds, about three miles away. He reconnoitered. He judged only two couples occupied the site. One couple was sleeping in a tent that opened up on the bed of a pickup. The other couple had erected a tent on the ground. Their campfire still smoldered.

Billy Leaps crawled over toward their fire. A frying pan rested beside the coals. That's what he'd take back as evidence of his infiltration. It seemed easy enough, and he was sure these people would have some other way to cook their food. He slithered across the clearing, moving in an unrhythmic fashion so that any sound he made would sound like a random forest noise.

He smiled to himself when he reached his destination, remembering to keep his lips tightly sealed so his teeth didn't show in the moonlight and give him away. He reached over and grabbed the handle of the frying pan.

A sudden and horrible pain shot through his right hand. He had misjudged. The pan was still on some of the coals. The fools hadn't taken it far enough from the fire, and it still burned with the heat. He should have known because he could still smell the smoking bacon grease inside it. He refused to admit defeat. He told the pain to go away. He dragged the hot pan after him. He would not leave it. He would certainly not admit the pain of the burning flesh on his hand.

As soon as he dared, he stood up and ran back to where there had been a pool of water. He dashed the pan and his hand into the pool. The pan hissed beneath the surface of the water. Steam rose off in the moonlight. "What an asshole," he murmured. "What a stupid, asshole mistake to make." He was furious with himself. How could he have made such an error?

He started to move back to the team's camp. Even as his hand throbbed with a dull pain, he decided he was glad to be reminded that he had to work just as hard as the rest of them. He wasn't a phys ed teacher for them. He was their team leader. And he had to be at peak just as much as they were. He was thirty-six years old now. He wasn't a kid. And he had forgotten things. After eight years you couldn't just pick up where you'd left off. That frying pan was important. It was a lesson he wanted never to forget. He almost hoped that there'd be a scar to remind him, always, every time he raised his hand to his face.

Cowboy brought back a pink toothbrush. "Too easy." He shrugged.

"Sometimes things work like a piece of cake," said Billy Leaps. "Just don't make the mistake of thinking they always will."

When the Greek arrived, he pulled a baseball cap out of his shirt. Beeker didn't need to ask whether or not Harry had gotten it off a man's head. He would have.

Rosie brought back a pair of sneakers. With socks inside them.

Applebaum came last, grinning triumphantly.

"Here's my trophy!" He lifted up a flesh-colored woman's bra.

"Did you get that off a line?" demanded Cowboy. "You were supposed to get in close to the camp, you jerk."

"She was *sleeping* in it!" protested Applebaum. He grinned again. "And she was dreaming in it. Dreaming about the man who was going to give her the fuck of her life."

"Oh, hell," Rosie said with disgust.

They moved about the bayous like that for days. Force marching, sleeping in quarter-hour snatches, trapped in their stinking clothes. They'd test themselves in strange ways. They'd come to a group of college kids out camping, and they'd all crawl at once toward them. Billy Leaps wanted to see how close they could get to unsuspecting civilians. They got very close.

Beeker made it seem real to them in ways that few drill instructors would even have thought about. He wanted them to remember the insufferable boredom of war. That was the thing these guys had learned from the Cong, what their own instructors had never taught them. To wait. To wait for hours and hours, and then to continue to wait longer. And to wait at peak.

If they came to any physical barrier, they had to act as if it were not here, in the southern part of Louisiana, but in Laos, or Cambodia. This had to be real or the exercise meant nothing. They crouched for hours by an Interstate highway waiting until there was no chance for traffic before Beeker would let them cross. Or, at another highway, he'd make them march an extra ten miles until they found a stream that had a tunnel—really just a drainpipe—underneath the roadbed. Then he made them crawl through the pipe on their backs while they held their guns over the vile, stagnant water.

They ate C rations and some dehydrated foods. He'd make them chow down while they were hiding only a few yards away from a country steak house. As they slowly devoured a tasteless, cold mixture of stringy beef and chunks of old potato meshed in a gelatinous pale gravy, they smelled the searing beef and baking potatoes in every breath they took. It was a simple exercise in denial, in not letting down their psychological guards.

But it got to them. Not the self-denial, not the physical brutality of the marches, but the sense that it wasn't real. That all of it was simply an elaborate exercise, of no more worth to the success of their mission than another thousand sets of leg presses would have been.

Billy Leaps decided he had to do something about that.

He would have to make it real.

13

In their marches through the countryside and the bayous of Louisiana, Beeker and his men had often come up suddenly on a gathering of oil wells, sluggishly but ceaselessly pumping up oil out of the ground with an enormous steel arm. In other places there were actual refineries, enormous surreal plants that spewed forth colored flames twenty-four hours a day. These wells and factories frequently stood in the middle of built-up swampland, their products sent out through huge pipelines to New Orleans and from there routed to other parts of the country. Their odors were noxious and seemed to comprise a constant possibility of explosion and death.

"I hate those things," Harry said when they stood in front of one of the solitary, small wells that are so often left completely untended. "You read the *Pentagon Papers* when they put them in the newspapers? I never bothered with the books, thought it'd just be more antiwar crap. But there the stuff was in the newspaper, so I read this one installment." He shook his head sadly. "You know what it said? The whole goddamn war was for oil. It was for oil rights off the coast of

Nam. All those people dead, all our goddamn friends dead—all that, for oil."

The others didn't respond. They simply stared at the well, its massive arm grinding away in its lopsided rhythm, beating at the ground like an imperturbable steel fist. They could smell the stink of the petroleum. This far away from civilization, and the place still smelled like they were standing on the edge of the Interstate. A little different because this oil wasn't refined, but the stink of it still covered that of the surrounding vegetation. Like the ultimate rot.

A few miles away was the refinery that accepted all the oil that was pumped out of the ground in the surrounding area. Billy Leaps took them there. They stood outside the fenced perimeter, staring up at the strange flames that burned off the waste material from the petroleum. The facility was enormous. A two-mile-long road connected the plant to the Interstate.

"All right," said Beeker, "no more toothbrushes and baseball caps. I want this plant."

His men stood stunned.

"You wanted a real test, right?" said Beeker. "Here it is. Think of this plant as an enemy fort. We have to secure the guards. However many there are."

"There's five," said Rosie. His reconnoitering had been automatic.

Beeker nodded approval.

"We can't off them," said Cowboy, a little uneasily.

"Why not?" demanded Applebaum with his usual enthusiasm and irrationality. "They deserve it." Harry's speech had stirred him up.

Beeker ignored the wiry blond man with the tattoo on his arm. "The plan is obvious. We figure out their shifts and their moments of greatest vulnerability, then we attack. We can't have any alarm sounded. We can't risk a counterattack. Because we're not going to have any guns. If they come together and understand what's happening to them, we could have our asses in slings from the fallout. They're armed, and they could come after us. And if we're caught, there'll be hell to pay. So this *is* real."

No one hesitated a moment. Beeker got a quick nod from every man. He made assignments. They patrolled the outskirts of the plant, carefully noting the time of arrivals and departures of various vehicles. Dozens of men and women went in and out of the plant's gates over the next twelve hours, all of them oblivious to the fact that five men, trained and outfitted for combat, watched their movements from light cover. People repeated Carson's jokes from the night before within earshot of Applebaum, who was daydreaming about the possible effects of his munitions against such a vulnerable target. With one grenade he could trigger an explosion that would be the top item on the evening's national news. Rosie thought of how the men and women presented themselves as such naked, obvious targets, standing unaware in little clusters in the yard of the plant, lounging by vending machines in open groups. Cowboy thought of the power of an air strike. Give him a gunship, and he could have the whole place in flames in a matter of half a minute or so.

They reconvened early in the evening just after the afternoon change in shift at the plant. They were intent on their business. It was no longer just a refinery belonging to the Intercontinental Pipeline Company. It was the enemy's stronghold.

"Their shift'll change again at eleven p.m.," said Beeker. "Let them do that, and let the new guards take their posts and get used to them. We'll attack just before one a.m." The word *attack* made them all sit up straighter, even more alert than before. "I want Rosie to take out the guy over here." Beeker was drawing a rough map of the plant in the dirt, using a pointed stick as a marker. "There are two other guard positions still open at night, both with two guards. Everything else gets closed down." He pointed again. "Cowboy, you and me will take this one. We'll work out the details later. Applebaum, you and Harry take this one." He pointed to the opposite side of the plant. "I want every guard to be out cold or tied up and blindfolded, gagged. I don't want anybody to hear one single sound come from their lips. But no damage, got it? No damage to the guards."

The men nodded.

"I will consider this mission a success if the guards are released tomorrow morning by the next shift. I don't want them getting loose by themselves. And I don't want them loose till we're long gone from here."

They broke up, the two double teams, and Rosie on his own.

Rosie's target was the only guard station with a single man in it. The other two stations were major entrances, but this one was only for pedestrians who came by bus and those who used the overflow parking lot farthest away from the plant.

He caught sight of his adversary through the wired-glass window of the guard station. Rosie was delighted with his draw. The man looked to be a worthy opponent. Black, like himself, the guard was bigger than Rosie. Taller and heavier. There'd be no way of knowing till the last minute if he was stronger. But strength wouldn't be the only determining factor, not even the most important. Rosie wasn't here to test his power; he was here to test his skill.

The minutes dragged on. The boredom deepened. The people who walked in and out of the gates in sudden waves around eleven o'clock seemed strange to Rosie now. He had so little in common with them. He listened carefully from his hidden vantage point, and he'd overhear their conversations, so innocent and detached from what might happen to them if Rosie chose. They weren't the Vietnamese considering the rice harvest; they were American factory workers talking about their kids, and football, and their illnesses. But the language still seemed foreign to Rosie.

Rosie thought about how lucky these factory workers were. How much luckier they were than the people in Nam who had no conception of what life was like free of the possibility of violence or attack. Those people over there had known what it was like to spend years with Americans, Australians, Koreans, Turks, VC, and their own soldiers constantly in the brush beside them. They were never shocked when a combat trooper stood up suddenly and waved a carbine at them. And for their parents, and their parents' parents, there had been waves of occupation and decades of fighting before that.

But what would these petroleum workers do if Rosie stood up now? His cammy-face and his shaved head and his M16 suddenly a part of the real world, not something to be seen in color on network television? What would these men and women say if they knew that five of the best-trained, most experienced soldiers in America were reconnoitering their plant at that very moment? What if they suddenly understood the potential violence that surrounded them?

As he crouched silently in the vegetation that bordered the plant property, Rosie felt a growing kinship with the guard he was going to take out. It was the same thing he had felt in Nam. Rosie had never made the mistake of thinking that the enemy was different from him. He wasn't. VC or NVN, it didn't make any difference: they were soldiers who were going to fight you, kill you if they had to—or could. Before skill, before luck, before anything else at all, it was will that was pitted against will. Rosie had known that, and that's why he was alive. Because he respected men who would do anything to survive.

The guard was one of those good men whom Rosie respected. He felt that. Rosie had an advantage because he was more prepared, he was more alert, he was the one who was going to attack. But the guard and his uniform weren't to be scoffed at. You don't scoff at anybody who carries a gun. You assume the man took the gun seriously and knew how to use it. Sure, Rosie could have picked him off with his M16. Rosie had marksmanship medals up the wazoo. But this was a silent attack, and Rosie was instructed to do no damage. That equalized things between the attacker and his intended victim.

But nobody had told the intended victim that he couldn't use his gun on Rosie. And that made the game very real.

I have only my hands and my head, thought Rosie.

Never attack on the quarter-hour, Beeker always said. It was expected. He had said: "Twelve fifty-three."

At twelve fifty Rosie moved. The guard was standing in the entranceway, his back against one of the steel fence posts. For some reason Rosie knew the man wanted a cigarette. There was a kind of tobacco jumpiness about him. He was obviously taking the enormous No Smoking sign seriously, though. Rosie could imagine what a single spark might do in a place like this.

The man's weapon was a pistol, holstered on his belt. His arms hung loosely beside him. His vigilance was sufficient to worry Rosie. Or was that vigilance just the nervousness of wanting a cigarette? Rosie had to assume the man was alert, not just nervy. Always give your adversary as much credit as possible. Give him the benefit of the doubt at all times, and maybe you could live. Underestimate his qualities for one second, on any point, and you might very well die for it.

Rosie knew he was only going to take the man out. He knew the man wasn't going to die. But the guard didn't understand that, he wouldn't know it was a game. He'd assume it was a real attack, real terrorists probably. Who else would be trying to break into a petroleum plant in the middle of the night?

The M16 would be useless. Rosie left it carefully on the ground. He crouched over and ran through the heavy underbrush till he was as close to the man as he could be and still remain under cover. A line of carelessly parked cars would be his next shield.

The boots would make noise on the gravel. Rosie untied them and took them off. In his stockinged feet he ran through the lot, never allowing his head to appear over the height of the cars' hoods. The gravel hurt. The small sharp stones cut into his feet. He had to ignore the pain. A little gravel was going to be the least of his problems in Laos; he knew that.

The guard's head seemed to be constantly turning. A couple of times Rosie thought he'd have been a dead man if the guard had been alert to the possibility of real danger. But he never expected that a man as well trained as Rosie was carefully, slowly making his way up the line of cars. He was only five feet away at one point. The guard made a mistake. He turned his head and seemed to be watching something inside the compound. Rosie checked his watch. It was exactly twelve fifty-three. Perhaps the guard's attention had been captured by some noise the other men had made. Rosie listened intently but heard nothing. And then all Rosie knew was that the man was making a mistake—he wasn't paying attention.

Without a sound Rosie dove. His head struck the guard's kidney and produced a gasp of intense pain and shock, but not enough noise to attract any attention. Rosie's hand went over the guard's mouth quickly and used the stifled jaw as a handhold. The guard bit the fleshy mound of Rosie's palm, but Rosie ignored the flash of pain. Rosie bounced the guard's head off the concrete pathway just once. All his muscles went lax at the same time. He was out cold.

Rosie hoped the blow wasn't sufficient to produce a

concussion. At least the guard was still breathing. Rosie unholstered the guard's pistol and tossed it over the fence into some shrubbery bordering the parking lot. Then he unlaced the man's shoes and used the leather cord to fasten the guard's arms behind him. He jerked the uniform trousers down to his ankles as bondage for the guard's legs. A handkerchief went into his mouth and was secured with the other shoelace. Then Rosie rolled the guard a few feet across the gravel, taking care of his head, and pushed him underneath a parked car. It would take him awhile to wake up, longer to crawl out from under the car, and then he'd have to wait for someone to come by and free him from the expertly applied ties.

Rosie did not even allow himself a moment of pleasure at his success. He quickly and quietly reclaimed his boots and his gun and disappeared into the underbrush once more. It was twelve fifty-eight.

A few minutes past one they were together again, every man grinning. Applebaum was jumping up and down, and Harry had to clamp a hand over his friend's mouth to keep him from shouting out loud.

Beeker led them quickly away from the plant.

Applebaum kept whispering, "We could've blown up the whole fucking state if we had wanted to. We are awesome!"

Beeker was less enthusiastic. "We did it right. But that's all. No more games now."

"We are awesome!" Applebaum made the words into a chant all the way back to Beeker's truck, seven or eight miles distant. He continued it as the other men stretched at full length on the harsh bed of the truck. The chant went on as Billy Leaps bounced the pickup over forest track and dirt roads, but then it was eventually lost to the wind when the truck pulled out onto the Interstate heading north to Shreveport.

14

The five men had begun to get on one another's nerves. It was inevitable; Beeker knew that. Combat troops at the peak of their training needed more than just a hundred more push-ups or a few dozen rounds on the rifle range to calm them down.

Applebaum was a natural lightning rod for the others. He'd kept talking, talking, yelling, yelling, bragging, bragging, detonating his explosives at strange times with too much enthusiasm. Already he'd torn up five sections of fence at the back of Billy Leaps's property. More than once the Indian had had to pull Cowboy or Rosie off the little blond man. He couldn't hold them together for much longer.

Beeker had called the number in D.C. every day for a week since they had returned from their training expedition in the south. A polite young woman took all his messages, but Parkes never called back. Beeker wondered if the publicity surrounding their training session had scared Parkes off. They hadn't been recognized—hell, they hadn't been seen—but the headlines in the New Orleans and Houston papers had produced a wave of paranoia across the oil-producing states. The stories had only infuriated Applebaum.

"We aren't leftist!" he screamed. "They're calling us communists. Hell, we aren't communists! I *kill* communists."

Beeker tried to explain. "Look, that's the only thing they can think of. Who else would do that to a petroleum plant? Besides, we did some good. Look how many men we got jobs for." The number of guards at the refineries in the Lake Charles area had been at least tripled since the attack. The media, and evidently the oil companies as well, had believed it to be a dress rehearsal for a real assault. Though why anyone would go so far and not carry through was a question no one could answer.

The men had resumed their training schedules, but it wasn't the same. The exercises meant nothing. They went through their routines with something like ease now—Beeker's men were that good. At the same time, they complained incessantly. Cowboy was the one who broke, finally.

"I have had it. I have fucking had it. Billy Leaps, you are team leader, you are chief, you are everything you fucking want to be. But I am bored. I am bored and I want to do something. You are running us like you used to run your rich kids at that snot-ass school. I don't need that. I love all you guys, but goddamn it, I need a woman. I need a woman real bad. I need to have me a good time, for Christ's sake!"

Billy Leaps knew the other men felt the same way. Who knew when Parkes would communicate with them? He couldn't keep his men bottled up forever. Better to let them blow off a little steam now.

"Okay," said Beeker. "We got plenty of money. What do you want to do?"

"Vegas," Cowboy replied without hesitation. "I want to go do Vegas. We got my plane right outside there. We can fly out tomorrow morning. We can blow it out there, just blow it out, and then we'll come right back. Promise, Beeker, then we can come back . . ."

"Or go on," Beeker said. "Okay. Vegas?" It was a question to the rest of them. They all agreed. "But take full packs; we got to be combat-ready. We might not be coming back here."

They moved quickly and efficiently. The boy watched them with a nervous eye. He wanted to know what was going to happen to him, but he didn't dare ask. Beeker saw his discomfort and finally took him aside. He sat on a wooden chair by the stove and looked at the kid.

"I need your help," he said. The boy responded with more nervousness. "I got to go for a while; it might be for a long while. I can't leave the farm empty, uncared-for. There's not much to do right now, it's not planting season yet, but I need the fire stoked so the pipes don't burst if there's a frost, and somebody's got to generally take care of things. Will you stay here for me?"

The boy smiled with relief and nodded yes. Beeker smiled and tousled his hair. "We got to get you back in school sometime, but it'll wait till I get back. Okay?"

The boy nodded again.

Beeker left the kid too much cash money and quickly ran over a list of things that had to be done around the place. The kid, obviously, couldn't use the telephone, but it was important that there be someone to guard the place. Or so Billy Leaps let the boy think.

Las Vegas is a totally artificial city, a tawdry glass jewel in the navel of the Nevada desert. It is built on land where there is no water and supports a population with no possibility of earning a living from any real labor. The sole industry is getting as much money as possible through the exploitation of human frailty. The town is a neon jungle of twenty-four-hour-a-day bars and gambling dens. A natural breeding ground for crime and corruption, it stands in stark contrast to everything that an American would want in a city. Yet it remains America's foremost playground. It's a cesspool in the sand, a place where values and social construction take a second place to instinct and greed.

They found a place to stay not far from the big hotels. A rented car would ferry them to the Hilton, the Riviera, and Caesars Palace.

Applebaum couldn't keep still and bounced up and down on the edge of the bed. "I want show girls. I want to see *flesh*. I want—"

"Shut up," Rosie sneered. "There is nothing but flesh in this place anyhow. This is the weirdest, most freaked-out town at night, like nothing *I've* ever seen. You been here before?"

"I've been everywhere," Applebaum boasted, his chin sticking out in a vain attempt to make his physical presence the match of Rosie's.

"Then you won't need me to tell you where to go to have a good time. Where to see the most flesh you can." Rosie grinned.

Applebaum was crestfallen. "Well, it's been a long time and—"

"Come on, guys," protested Cowboy, "we got to start at the Hilton, we just got to."

The five toured many of the hotels the first day. They quickly sank into the strangeness of Las Vegas, a place where nothing closes, where daylight seems like an arbitrary natural phenomenon, not anything by which to regulate your life. Women are on the street prostituting themselves at dawn, people eat when their stomachs tell them they have to, and restaurants serve breakfast to accompany the evening news. The slot machines provide a background of metallic music, the Las Vegas equivalent to choirs singing. Money is the undisguised religion of the place, and everybody is a worshipper.

Beeker's men loved the place. They loved the weirdness of it. Women in only the tiniest triangles of spangled cloth marched through the casinos pushing tobacco, booze, anything that would keep the men throwing their chips on the gaming tables. Applebaum was in heaven. His bloated ego led him to throw piles of chips on the constantly losing numbers of the roulette wheel, and the women would respond immediately by buying him a drink on the house, letting him grab hold of their beautiful bodies while the management looked on from above and smiled at their good work.

Cowboy played just as relentlessly as Applebaum, but Cowboy had built-in restrictions that saved him from the financial devastation that the little man went through. Cowboy got some winners. He was able to maintain his pile of chips at a fairly constant level. As time went on, it got a little smaller and a little smaller, but that, Cowboy considered, was only paying for his fun. The girls liked men from Texas, and Cowboy's hat and mirrored glasses made him look like the real thing. He got the women he needed so much, but kept himself down to just one a day—so he could concentrate on what he was doing, he explained to Billy Leaps.

Rosie was a little more work for the girls. They knew their business. They knew that you could give a man like Applebaum the barest hint of conquest and he'd feel like a king. But a man like Rosie, that was different, and their professional knowledge kept them distant from him. He would expect something, they knew that, and they weren't at all sure they wanted to deliver it. Not sure at all.

And Harry? Harry just drank. A slow but constant river of alcohol. The girls knew his kind too. He was another one they didn't care to be around, at least not unless they were hard enough to look into the eyes of a desperately lonely man, a man whose pain was evident whenever he looked at a beautiful woman. Some other beautiful woman had done something to Harry, something that he had never forgotten, and no female employee of the casino wanted to be the one to remind him of it.

So the scantily clad women responded to the men individually, with their sharply learned lessons from years on the gaming floors. It was a joy to have such easy work as Applebaum. Cowboy was fun. Rosie and the Greek they tended to avoid. But it was Billy Leaps they wanted.

The women would glance over at the tall tanned-faced man and see something in him—was it just because of that strange mangled ear?—that made juices flow. The women on the floor of the casinos always made exceptions. And in Billy Leaps they saw the one they would break all the rules for.

Billy Leaps ignored them. He was preoccupied with the phone call he made every morning and every afternoon. The result was always the same. Parkes wasn't in.

Cowboy knew that Billy Leaps would never enjoy Las Vegas. It was the last place in the world that a man like him would have a good time. But the sinking expression on the Indian's face wasn't because of his displeasure with the city; it had much more to do with those unanswered telephone messages. Cowboy finally spoke to Billy Leaps about it. "What's the worst that can happen? Parkes never contacts us. Big deal. We got his money."

"The money is nearly gone," Billy Leaps said. They were in the hotel room they shared. Beeker was looking at the pastel painted walls with the manufactured "art" firmly attached to keep it from being stolen. Everything was possible in Las Vegas. Nothing was sacred but profit and pleasure.

"We've always landed on our feet, Beeker. We'll manage again. It was enough to get us all together again. It was more than enough to get through the training. Yeah, it ragged me, it got me real burnt up, but it was good."

"It's not enough to be weekend soldiers," Beeker said. "It's been much more than that. We got more than a chance to playact." He continued to stare at the wall. But his expression wasn't blank, it was clearly and sharply focused. "We got to see too much."

"Too much of what?"

"Too much of ourselves. Being a soldier again. The uniforms. This is who we are, Cowboy, this is who we have to be." He stood up suddenly and slammed a fist into the wall. "And we're dependent on a fuck-up like Parkes. There are supposed to be eighteen American men in a POW camp in Laos. We are trained to rescue them. We're veterans. We know the place and the enemy. We should be there now. But we have to wait for a fucking phone call from a desk jockey in Washington to move."

Parkes wasn't at his desk that afternoon either. The receptionist took Beeker's message as if there weren't a stack of them a foot high on her desk already. That night Billy Leaps wandered about the enormous gambling room of the Hilton. He watched Cowboy's easy way of keeping his head above water and Applebaum's lunatic way of drowning himself.

When he looked about the room, he was disgusted, not at the pursuit of idle, vicious pleasure, but at his own enforced inactivity. He could do nothing without Parkes, and that made him very angry.

When the woman came up to him, he assumed she was another shill for the hotel. She was a beautiful blonde with creamy skin and impossibly blue eyes. Her body was impossible as well. Impossibly beautiful. She stood in front of him with an unlighted cigarette to her lips.

"No matches," said Beeker, unapologetically.

She smiled at his stoic responses. She wasn't used to such lack of interest from men.

"There are matches in the lounge," she replied. "Drinks too. I could use one of each."

"Sorry," said Billy Leaps and started to turn away. But the woman swiftly grabbed his hand. He felt something between their palms, a rectangle of stiff paper. She withdrew her hand and turned away with a smile. She walked into the lounge. Billy Leaps looked at what she had left in his hand.

It was a photograph of his friend Gougelmann.

They sat together at a tiny table in the lounge. Her name was Delilah, and she looked with curiosity but no discomfort at his mangled ear. He lighted her cigarette. She stared past him into the casino area. Applebaum still stood at the roulette wheel with a meager pile of chips, and Harry—nearly incoherent with drink—stood beside him.

"I thought you were supposed to be in training," she said softly. The waiter brought their drinks. She smiled at Billy Leaps. He fished money for the drinks out of his pocket.

"We are," said Billy Leaps. "They're blowing off steam."

"How do *you* blow off steam?" Delilah asked.

Billy Leaps ignored the question.

"Where's Parkes?" he demanded.

Delilah shrugged and smiled. "I don't know anybody called Parkes."

"Where did you get the picture?"

She shrugged again and said, "You won't get anywhere asking me questions. Why don't you just listen to what I have to say?"

Billy Leaps sat back. He had ordered himself a bottle of beer. It cost four dollars.

"Your plane leaves LAX for Bangkok in three hours," Delilah said.

Billy Leaps covered his surprise with silence.

"So you don't have much time. You can either fly from here to LAX in Mr. Hatcher's plane, or there's a commercial flight leaving in three quarters of an hour." She glanced toward the gaming room. "I would suggest you take the commercial flight. Mr. Hatcher's had his share of bourbon this afternoon, I think."

Beeker didn't hesitate. "Cowboy will fly us to L.A."

The woman smiled vaguely. "The plane's been refueled. It's all set. So I would suggest that you gather up your men, Mr. Beeker."

She stood up, and Beeker followed her movement a second later.

"Parkes—" he began.

"I told you," Delilah said, "I don't know anybody called Parkes. Your bags have already been packed. They're waiting for you in a limousine outside. License plate, Nevada Hackney 1233. The driver will have your Bangkok tickets. And some new identification. You've just become Mr. Baker and associates, and you're interested in cheap labor for the manufacture of textiles. I hope you and your friends have a pleasant time in Bangkok, Mr. Baker."

15

When the 747 began its descent into Bangkok, the five men cheered. Just to get out of that flying box of metal and plastic and onto the ground was going to be a great relief, they all thought. A trans-Pacific flight was the worst place in the world to try to sober up after a three-day binge.

The enormous wheels hit the pavement, and the jet went through its loud mechanical braking. Quickly it quieted down, and again the engines drove them toward the waiting terminal. They obediently lined up with the other passengers and waited for the door to open.

They could identify him from the top of the metal gangway. "Asshole," Applebaum said. Their contact was wearing the uniform of the CIA—the business suit that no real businessman ever wore, the light blue shirt, the dark tie not too narrow and not too wide, a facade which tried so hard to be innocuous and overlookable that it seemed fairly to scream, *Look at me! Look at me!* Just like in Saigon, the CIA operatives were as obvious as it was possible to be while they played their games at intrigue and spying.

MICHAEL MCDOWELL AND JOHN PRESTON

The man walked right up to Billy Leaps. "Martinsdale," he said robustly, pumping Beeker's hand.

Beeker made no response. They all had names like that.

"Your baggage has been transferred to the next domestic flight to Ubon Ratchathani. Your flight's a little late. We have to go right to the gate."

"No way," complained Harry, who alone of his friends hadn't needed to sober up on the plane. Harry never got hangovers, and he was still full of the free first-class booze. "I want Bangkok for a while. Best R and R I ever had was here. I want to go into the city. Least till we get ourselves geared to the time changes."

The CIA man said simply, "The plane leaves in five minutes." He turned and walked away.

"Let's go," said Billy Leaps with no enthusiasm. Martinsdale was an underling of Parkes. That made him, by simple logic, a fuck-up, and an untrustworthy fuck-up at that. The Cherokee didn't like following a man like that anywhere, even to the other side of an airport. But there was nothing else to do.

The 727 that would fly them to Ubon Ratchathani was a lot different from the 747 that had brought them across the Pacific, where their fellow passengers had been international businessmen or wealthy travelers. The people who crowded on this second-leg plane were from all classes. Civil servants, Thai soldiers, petty Japanese businessmen, and peasants who looked so poor you wondered how they ever scrounged up the fare. Cowboy said it was like a backwoods bus, something that plied the milk route from Pascagoula to Natchez.

The smells assaulted the men. The alien spices in the clothes and the skin of the Orientals brought back Vietnam. The voices that were at once guttural and sharp and seemed barely capable of communicative speech made them realize that they were a long way from Louisiana.

Billy Leaps sat beside the CIA man. They didn't exchange a word the entire flight. Beeker knew his companion would not allow any talk of their mission. Martinsdale would look at the Japanese salesman across the aisle and see a paid informer. He'd want to believe that the six-member Thai family making such a racket behind them with their quick, high-noted voices were cleverly disguised enemy agents. Probably—and this more than anything kept Billy Leaps quiet—the CIA man would know the acronyms for the intelligence and counterintelligence agencies for every single country in the western Pacific. The last thing Beeker wanted to do was listen to that obnoxious listing of initials that meant so much to people in the CIA and were just levels of bullshit to men like Beeker.

Billy Leaps kept his eyes closed for most of the trip. He just let the sounds and the smells wash over him. He waved away a harried stewardess when she tried to serve a snack on the short hop.

Then he felt the plane descending. He sat up. He didn't have to understand the orders that came over the loudspeaker in Thai: *Please fasten your safety belt* . . . It was the same anywhere.

The plane landed smoothly and then taxied to the hangar. Ubon Ratchathani didn't have the gleaming international terminals that Bangkok had put up for the tourists and international businessmen. It was a small provincial city. Beeker watched the building grow larger. It wasn't too different from the one in Shreveport. Little city, out of the way, a place where no one would notice if a stranger disappeared.

Or five strangers.

The doors were open, and a sudden wave of heat swept through the cabin. The heat. He had actually forgotten the heat. He looked around and caught Cowboy's eyes. Each knew what the other was thinking. The bayous had been child's play. They were back in a part of the world where a ten-degree change in temperature made little difference. The human body can't register the climb from 98 degrees to 110. It can only register heat, scarcely bearable, sometimes deadly, always miserable heat. They had lived in this heat for years. It had been their steady companion, as dependable as death, as constant as killing. They were back in the heat of Southeast Asia.

Beeker and his team walked down the steps and onto the tarmac. The hot surface cooked the soles of their feet. The air conditioning of the terminal was no more than a futile gesture, like an arm raised to ward off a bullet. As soon as they had claimed their bags, they were back outside and into a taxi. The CIA man gave the driver some orders, and he sped away into the city.

They dropped their luggage and gathered in the room assigned to Billy Leaps. Martinsdale was already waiting for them. He had ordered drinks in a patent attempt to insinuate himself. Under Billy Leaps's unspoken signal, all the men took either mineral water or orange juice. There was no knowing how soon they'd see combat. Las Vegas and its indulgences were far behind them now.

The room was not air-conditioned. The dark stains of perspiration were already spreading out from their armpits on their civilian clothes. Their slacks clung to their buttocks with the perspiration dampness.

Martinsdale had a large portfolio with him, like one an art student might use to carry his work in. He placed it against the head of one of the twin beds, discarding a pillow onto the floor. He unzipped the case and pulled out a stack of oversized photographs. He propped the first photograph against the headboard. "I'm told you know this man."

It was Gougelmann, the same photograph Delilah had handed to Beeker, but considerably enlarged.

Beeker's men stared silently at the photograph. They had all known Gougelmann.

"These are the others." Slowly, Martinsdale raised seventeen more photographs and propped them one by one in front of Gougelmann's picture. He gave each man a name, military status, and date of supposed capture. One of the men, an Army corporal, had been in enemy hands for eleven years.

"Eighteen men," said Martinsdale solemnly. "In the hands of an especially radical communist group. They operate in Laos now, after having been driven out of Cambodia a few years ago. For all practical purposes they rule this area of the country."

The CIA agent righted a map of the Indochinese peninsula. All five men knew the map from memory. They stared at the red square marked near the Laotian border with Thailand. "Our latest intelligence reports say the enemy is operating in this particular sector right now." On a second, more detailed map, he pinpointed one Laotian river valley that lay parallel to the Mekong, but about forty kilometers to the east of the Thai border.

"Why haven't Gougelmann and the others been brought out before now?" asked Beeker.

"The complexities of the political situation in this part of Asia have not simplified in the past few years. If anything, they've become even more garbled since the Cambodian revolution and the Vietnamese response to it. We only very recently discovered the existence of these captives."

"How?"

Martinsdale hesitated only briefly. "The group contacted us directly. They want a deal. Certain arms. Arms in return for the eighteen men. We couldn't do it. The arms would have been used against our allies. Right now we're still in negotiations. Holding them off until you people get in there."

"Why didn't you just give them the fucking arms?" said Rosie. "Just because they're the enemy—that never stopped us before." He remembered the times when various factions or tribes would turn their U.S. weapons on the Saigon government while American troops watched, horrified at the loss of allies, the waste of material, the added danger that Indochinese infighting brought to the war.

Martinsdale replied stiffly: "We cannot deal directly with an organization that is so directly opposed to our strategic needs."

"Cut the shit," said Harry, impatiently. "Let's get on to the real stuff."

Martinsdale looked grossly offended. He glanced at the team leader. Billy Leaps nodded. "Get on with it. We don't care about Agency politics in this."

"It's quite simple, actually," said Martinsdale urbanely. "Go in. Knock out the troops guarding the POWs. Get them out. Come back here."

Martinsdale's high-handedness was insulting, but Beeker ignored it. He merely asked, "Why aren't you using Montagnards?" He had wondered why the old allies of the Americans, the deadly local killers of Vietnam, weren't the ones for this particular operation. The Montagnards were already trained; they knew the area better than any Americans ever would; they would be easier to get in and get out.

"We don't trust any of the groups currently operating in Indochina," returned the CIA man shortly.

"They don't trust you," Cowboy corrected. Nearly every promise the CIA had made in Southeast Asia in the past quarter century had been broken. More than that, the CIA had turned against every ally it had ever had there, at one point or another. Who would trust Martinsdale? Or any of the hundreds like him?

"Look," said Martinsdale with exasperation, "I'm your contact. I don't have to take any of this . . ." He suddenly seemed to recover himself. He turned his face away from them and pointed to the map once more. "You pick up your supplies here." He pointed to a tiny *X* just over the Laotian border.

"You want us to go into Laos *unarmed*?" Applebaum was the first to yell in disbelief. The others seconded him with quieter murmurs.

"You're in Thailand now. One of few allies left to us. We can't have American mercenaries—"

"*Mercenaries!*" Rosie screamed in anger.

"We weren't answering blind ads in the fucking classifieds!" said Cowboy in disgust.

"Mercenaries . . . !" breathed Harry in disgust, exchanging murderous looks with Applebaum.

"We didn't get here on our own, you know," said Beeker with quiet disdain. "So far as we're concerned, this is a CIA contract operation."

"No, no, it isn't," stammered Martinsdale. "Obviously it isn't. Obviously we can't own you if something goes wrong. I mean, we paid for your training. And we've put money in your accounts, but this isn't our operation. Not an Agency operation at all. We're just coordinating. We're—"

Beeker cut him off in disgust. The CIA took credit only when a mission was successful; everybody knew that. And they were democratic—they'd take credit for anything, from anybody. "We sent a list of supplies ahead of us. I sent it to Parkes weeks ago. The bare essentials. We will not go into Laos without them."

Martinsdale seemed relieved to have the subject changed. "You have your supplies," he said. "Inside Laos." He pointed to the map again. "They're right here. One kilometer inside the border. You cannot have that kind of armament in Thailand. It's impossible."

"It's impossible for us to cross a hostile border without them. That's final."

Martinsdale was distressed. When he spoke, it was with unexpected sincerity. You could hear a chain of command behind him. He was following someone else's instructions. "I just couldn't get all the stuff you requested inside Thailand. It would have meant involving the Thai military, the Thai foreign service, all of them. They're clean right now; they're trying to work by the book. They simply are not going to let foreign troops go into Laos without their knowledge and direction."

Rosie reached into his pocket and produced his ticket envelope. "I knew there was a reason I loved the phrase 'round trip.'"

Martinsdale looked away for a moment. "I can get you rifles. M16s. That's what you're used to, right?"

"Anybody can get hold of a fucking M16," said Harry in disgust. "But I got to have *my* M16. You think I'm going to trust a piece that comes out of God knows nowhere?"

This wasn't precisely true, but Harry felt that he and the others had been betrayed by Martinsdale, and he was determined to give the agent a hard time.

Martinsdale seemed to give in. "Your own equipment was taken out of your Beechcraft at LAX. We can have it brought over here by diplomatic pouch. You'll have that by midnight tomorrow," he conceded.

Beeker thought for a moment. He turned to the others. "What do you think?"

"M16s are the cake," said Harry. "If they're ours, that is. The rest of it's frosting. We know we can go anywhere with the rifles."

"Christ!" exclaimed Martinsdale, who was sweating

profusely. "You only have to go a fucking kilometer into Laos. All the rest of your stuff is there, waiting for you. Every goddamn thing on that list."

"We have no reason to believe that," said Beeker coldly. "We have no reason to believe anything you've told us. Just get us what we brought from Louisiana, and we'll go in."

Martinsdale capitulated with a sullen nod.

16

Thailand's darkness surrounded them. Asian nights have a different quality entirely from the nights in the Western Hemisphere. They are deep, sinister, timeless. An Indochina night can make you forget there is such a thing as day.

They had made their way out of Ubon Ratchathani at midnight. Beeker's men sat on the floor in the back of the van, trying not to feel ridiculous as they bounced along in a vehicle properly registered and inscribed with the name of a television distributor on its sides.

"Great cover," Martinsdale had bragged. No one seconded his complacency.

Beeker sat up front with the CIA agent, ostensibly to follow the map with a flashlight. That wouldn't be needed, of course. Billy Leaps took one glance at the map, noted where they were, marked their destination, checked the roads in between, then folded and put the map away.

Martinsdale was impressed. And annoyed. But the map business was only a ruse anyway. He needed to talk to the team leader. The Thai highways were potholed, two-laned affairs, often completely overhung with vegetation and inky black at night. The drive toward the Laotian border was slow and tedious.

"You've got quite a group back there," Martinsdale said, cocking his head over his shoulder. "They're everything I was told they would be."

"What's that?" Beeker's interest was pricked.

"Combat veterans. Rough stuff. Hard core." Martinsdale may have wanted a round of agreement, but he didn't get it. He got silence. "I really know a lot about you," he added when Beeker didn't respond.

Beeker knew better than to ask questions when it was apparent that Martinsdale wanted nothing more than to be drawn out. He'd let the CIA man braid his own hanging rope.

"You and your men have amazing records," Martinsdale went on, a smile creeping onto his face. Billy Leaps could just see the glint of his teeth in the reflected light from the dashboard of the vehicle. "Never saw so many commendations and medals in my life. All kept secret of course. Too bad you guys had to miss out on the ceremonies. Those ceremonies can mean a lot to a guy. But you know what's the most amazing thing about your war records?"

Martinsdale wasn't watching the road, and the right front tire fell into a deep pothole. The truck lurched, and the CIA man jerked the wheel to the right to avoid getting the back tire in as well.

Beeker didn't bother making a reply to Martinsdale's remark. He knew that Martinsdale had something to say and that he'd say it.

"The most amazing thing about your records is that they don't exist."

Beeker could feel the sense of power in Martinsdale's voice.

"Every single piece of paper with your name on it has been

destroyed. Commendations, medals—you guys will never get hold of those. Enlistment forms—gone. Fingerprints—burned up. You name it." Martinsdale chuckled. "It's not there anymore. You five guys are nonmen. Unveterans. You're lucky they let you keep hold of your social security numbers. If they did. Any of you guys applied for credit lately?"

Billy Leaps felt uneasy. The CIA could have done it, he knew that, but they would have had to work hard at it. And why would they have wanted to? That was the question. He had the feeling that Martinsdale had just told him more than it was good for him to know—from the CIA's point of view of course. Beeker still said nothing, hoping that Martinsdale would spit up something else.

"Of course it's not really burned up, it's just been pulled. Langley has it. They're storing it. And if you do a good job over here, if you go in there and get what we want and bring it out again, then maybe those papers will get put back in their proper places. You understand me?"

So, the CIA was just doing a little advance covering-up in case something went wrong with the mission. That's obviously what Martinsdale thought. But maybe there was something else behind it, something Martinsdale himself didn't suspect. Billy Leaps thought there was, and he tried to puzzle it out.

Martinsdale was annoyed that his gibes seemed to have no effect on the man beside him. Billy Leaps discouraged further conversation by saying, "Watch the road, Martinsdale. If the five of us are going to die, I'd just as soon it wasn't in a goddamn television truck."

Martinsdale missed his turn off despite Billy Leaps's warning that it was coming up. He had to back up a quarter of a mile on the narrow highway and then turn off onto a jungle back road. They traveled along it as far as the encroaching vegetation would allow, and then Martinsdale halted the truck. Billy Leaps was already out, however. He went around the back, opened the doors, and said quietly, "This is it."

The four men climbed out with their duffel bags. They arranged themselves a few feet apart on the parallel tracks of the jungle road they had just come along and drew out the clothing that had become so much a part of them during their training. Martinsdale had come around with a large flashlight, and was beaming it over the men, watching incredulously as they stripped down and redressed, without a word, in absolute quiet. When he turned the flashlight off, the CIA agent heard nothing but the noises of the jungle around him.

Beeker and his team dressed into the fatigues black-side out. Martinsdale shone the flashlight again, curiously watching the men apply the black grease to one another's faces. He saw Beeker put a covering of the stuff on the top of the black man's head. Martinsdale could have sworn that it had just been shaved that night. The black man had had some hair yesterday, he was sure of it. But now, until Beeker had layered the dull paste on it, the large black skull with the tiny white skull earring had glistened whenever the flashlight swept across it.

The men inspected one another, making sure that the back of everyone's neck was camouflaged, the telltale inches of white flesh on Applebaum and Cowboy not showing between shirt and pants. The agent was stupefied by the coordination of it all. Where had he seen such intense, automatic, silent preparation before? It brought back some vague memory. He had seen men operate this way when he was a child—the silent movements, the inherent knowledge of what was needed, and the agreement on how it was to be done. These men were getting ready to enter Laos, a country with a government that was fragmentary, garbled, dangerous. Anything might happen to them there. Martinsdale tried to think of situations he had witnessed in Vietnam to come up with the equivalent to this. His mind drew a blank.

Then he remembered.

He was a small boy in Ohio, and one day he watched the priests and acolytes of St. John the Divine's Church preparing for mass. They had moved just like this. The only other time Martinsdale had seen men interact in this way, in this spirit, was in the preparation for the holiest ceremony of the church.

But these men were going to war.

He was shaken by the recollection. It took a few moments to take in Billy Leaps's words, spoken in a low voice, directly in his ear. "Shine the light in the back of the van."

Beeker and Rosie unloaded their meager supplies. They had exactly what they had taken with them into the Louisiana bayous. No more, no less. At least in that, the CIA had not let them down. They had brought the stuff over in less than eighteen hours and gotten it into Thailand in a diplomatic pouch. Martinsdale had seemed proud of his work in this, but Beeker pointed out that it was still a great deal less than they had been promised originally.

Martinsdale angrily reiterated: "Your stuff is over there, Beeker. Every goddamn cartridge, every goddamn grenade, every goddamn ration you put down."

Beeker shrugged noncommittally.

The men were checking their rifles. Martinsdale could hear, but he could see nothing. Beeker's men and Beeker himself were working in pitch darkness, smoothly, without hesitation. They gauged each bolt action, tested each grip, ran their fingers over the ammunition pouches they fastened over their shoulders—all in darkness.

"You did all that before you got in the van," Martinsdale complained. "And how can you do it in the dark anyway?"

"In Nam," said Beeker, speaking as he bolted and unbolted the rifle several times in quick succession, "and in boot camp before Nam, we learned to make love to an M16."

"But in the dark?" Martinsdale continued to protest.

"Can you take a shit in the dark?" came Applebaum's voice, full of sarcastic contempt.

"Of course . . ." answered Martinsdale weakly.

"Well then," said Cowboy, "why don't you go do that, and leave us alone?"

The men all laughed, all except Martinsdale of course. He wasn't used to being treated this way. He didn't like it. He experienced—for the first time—the deep awareness that he was unlike them. He understood also that he would never be like them. He was frightened now to be so close, so near five men who were never going to be either his friends or his tools, neither his to manipulate nor his to order about. They seemed inhuman. He wondered whether they had been born that way, whether it was training that did it to them, or whether it was on account of what they had experienced in Vietnam. Probably a little of all three.

The five men were ghostlike. They seemed at ease in the jungle, as if they'd come fifteen years before and never left it. They stood with their faces blackened and their uniforms so dark that Martinsdale could see only their outlines. That and the whites of their eyes or their teeth when they spoke. He wondered that he had dared to say to Beeker, "You don't exist." And he wondered whether he might have spoken a truth greater than he had known.

He sensed their readiness, though still they did not speak to him.

"Everything's in order. Right through there"—he pointed

and wondered if they could even see him in such darkness—"there's a sampan waiting to take you across the Mekong. The arms cache is one kilometer south-south-east from there."

One of them asked—Martinsdale didn't know which one—"Is this how you plan for us to get back across?"

"Yeah," said another one. "With us, Gougelmann, and seventeen others?"

There was more contempt in their voices. It was as if they didn't believe in the plan that had been set up. But if they didn't believe in it, why were they here? Why were they going through with it? The CIA agent didn't understand at all.

"Plans have been made," said Martinsdale. "There's a PRC-10 with your supplies. You just say 'black, black,' and evac choppers will take you out. They'll tell you where the PZ is."

He climbed into the truck, and backed hurriedly along the path.

Beeker and his men were left alone in the Thai jungle. When the noise of the truck subsided, they could hear again the flow of the river water beyond the trees. They went that way and after some little searching found a stoic Chinaman waiting with the sampan that Martinsdale had promised.

At this point the Mekong River is wide, slow-moving, and black. It smelled different here than it did in the Delta. Still it was the same river. And they felt for the Mekong what Mark Twain felt for the Mississippi: it was the river of their dreams. Only their dreams were usually nightmares.

"I'm surprised he didn't want us just to swim across. And carry a couple of mail pouches while we were at it," said Cowboy. "Something's wrong, Beeker."

One man spoke for all. It had been that way for a while. They all sensed something off, about Martinsdale, about the mission.

"You think we've been shafted?" Harry wanted to know. "You think it's Parkes again?"

Billy Leaps knew better than to try to calm his men with assurances he himself didn't feel. He never lied to them. He was their leader, but he was also part of the team. They deserved the truth.

Billy Leaps said, "I don't know. Something does feel wrong. I don't trust Martinsdale. Not an inch. And I've never trusted Parkes. But we're going on."

They crossed the river in silence. As soon as they had landed, the Chinaman silently poled his sampan away from the shore and soon was lost to their sight and hearing.

They began their march through the jungle at a little past two a.m. Beeker was at point, leading the way. He had a compass and had memorized the location of the ammunition dump. Five minutes got them there.

But they had been able to smell it beforehand. The stink of expended powder. The smoke was still rising from the gnarled metal. A small scrub tree was sullenly burning at the edge of the pile. What had been rifles and grenades, ammunition and mortar shells, provisions and clothing, was now a pile of melted, charred waste.

There wasn't one of the men who hadn't expected this, in his heart. Expected it from the moment that Martinsdale had said, "Your supplies are over the border in Laos."

They did not go near. Whoever had done this might still be around. Beeker whispered, "We go on."

The four men under him paused a moment, and in silence the decision was made among them. Harry spoke for the group. "I told you the M16s were the cake. All that would have been frosting. Just frosting."

Their destination was another five-hour march. Beeker

checked his compass once more, and then led them off deeper into the jungle.

Memories came with the heat. The constant sweating. Rosie reached into his pack and chewed on a piece of plastic till he got to his salt tablets. And this was only the night. He dreaded the heat of the day and the morning's unrelenting sun. Those fucking salt tablets had been a constant, unvarying part of his life in Nam, and here he was again, with the same acridity burning his gums.

Cowboy used his memories to get through the forced march. He had to think of other things. He hated being on the ground, out of his element. It made him feel open to attack. Where was a plane? A copter? He was a flyer, not an infantry man. He knew the goddamn M16, of course. And he cradled it nearly as lovingly as Beeker himself. But what he really wanted was to get his hands on a Huey. All that power in his hands. In the air Cowboy was in control. And when a man was in control, he could do anything.

Their memories got them through the jungle. Every man with his own. It all came back clearly, and all their responses to their environment were automatic. It was nothing like the bayous—this Laotian jungle made the bayous seem as harmless as a Disneyland rain forest—but strangely enough, Beeker and his men felt more at home here. If home was ever a living hell.

Their alertness came easily, without their forcing it. By automatic consent they gripped their M16s and followed in a line spread out enough that one shell couldn't get all of them. They were able to avoid the villages because they could sense the clusters of huts and smell the deadened fires long before they had reached them. They marched around the villages. Without thinking.

Beeker barely felt the need to consult his compass.

Everything was memorized. As much as Cowboy and his flying skill, Billy Leaps trusted in his scouting. It seemed as though he had marched through this jungle all his life. It was almost as familiar to him as the ranges of Oklahoma where he had grown up and played frontier games with neighbor kids. He anticipated every ravine, expertly gauged the depth of every stream, knew exactly when they should try to find a shallower ford and when going farther out of the way would be pointless.

Yet the team had more visceral reactions as well. Rosie needed to piss. He needed to piss bad. But he knew to wait for one of those river crossings before he released a stream of urine. The feel of the warm flowing water was as effective a trigger now as the sound of a john flushing had been a few weeks ago.

They experienced things they'd thought they'd never have to know about again. The squirming of leeches as they tried to burrow deeper into their clothing. The men didn't even try to fight them off. There'd be no way to. The leeches could be removed only with fire or bug juice. The bug juice went up with the dump. Now they couldn't light so much as a single match. It could be their deaths. So the leeches that did fight their way down to the skin stayed there, for an uninterrupted feast on the men's blood. But Beeker and Beeker's men had spent whole days with leeches sticking to them. That had been years before, but you don't forget something like that. Not ever.

They continued their march through the jungle.

17

The night seemed to end without warning. Suddenly light poured down from above, and steam rose up from the ground below. They traveled for an hour in the light. They reached their destination without warning to them. All night long they had tramped through heavy undergrowth and slogged through sullen streams, passing only occasionally very crudely cleared fields of manioc or rice. Now, suddenly, they found themselves on a little rise overlooking what looked to be several hundred acres of carefully and professionally tended fields.

The flowers were gone. They didn't need to see the flowers to know what sort of crop had been grown there. The flowers were poppies, and the crop was opium. Poppies into opium, opium into heroin, heroin into the streets of Detroit, Chicago, New York, Seattle, and St. Louis. They were looking at Death's Meadows.

"I was here before," said Harry softly, standing beside Beeker behind cover of a dense thicket unruffled by any cooling breeze. "This whole area was devastated. We lost hundreds of men here. We fought that fucking war for democracy, for the wonderful peoples of Southeast Asia, for fucking apple pie and mom. It's ten years later and what do we get? Three hundred acres of poppies."

"The Memorial Day flower," sneered Applebaum. He sat on the ground and was pulling off his boots. They were filled with blood—the work of the leeches. "Pretty red flowers. Blood red."

The men stared out at the unpeopled vista. They were a quarter of a mile away, but their view was clear. Billy Leaps spread out the map.

"You can see the big house from here." He pointed over to the other side of the fields. "It's one of those old colonial plantation things the French built. Their compound is structured around it." He took out field glasses and scanned quickly. Nodding, he said, "Looks straight to me. They got that right. If we can't trust Parkes, and we can't trust Martinsdale, maybe we can at least trust their map."

He held the map up before him and glanced over the edge of it at the house and fields it represented, checking for accuracy. His men stood silently behind him, hidden at the verge of the forest.

"Cowboy, you move along this side." Billy Leaps indicated the flank that appeared least fortified and the least likely to afford them all entry. It wasn't a put-down to give Cowboy this particular assignment, just the recognition that of all of them he was the least accustomed to ground combat.

"Rosie, you and me'll take the other side. Harry and Applebaum, right up the middle. I want Cowboy to open up on the house as the two teams move in from different directions. Real simple. Move in shooting. Fast and hard and accurate. If we run out of ammo, there's no backup."

"How many you think there are?" Rosie wanted to know.

"Martinsdale said twenty-five. Seems right for the size of

the place. Might be less since the flowers have already been harvested. They'll probably have moved the field hands on already. Leaving some command types behind, just to guard the prisoners." He stood up, and the rest did the same.

"Check your watches. I got six-o-seven."

Only Rosie made a slight adjustment.

"We should all be inside in half an hour," said Beeker. "Dusk is as good as dawn, you can move in the shadows. Let's go."

They moved cautiously through the underbrush and down along the perimeter of the well-tended fields. The first crop of flowers had been harvested, but a few had bloomed since, and even these few blossoms were enough to weight the air with their sickly sweet odor. Beeker had heard about women and men who worked the poppy fields getting stuck on the stuff just from inhaling the fragrance of the flowers for so long.

"Hey, man," said Rosie cautiously, "I'm getting a buzz on. Billy Leaps, pick it up, pick it up."

Beeker did pick up the speed. He wondered who the field workers had been: the Cambodians' own men, hired women from the neighboring villages perhaps, or just nameless slaves culled from five nations, a hundred tribes, a thousand villages. At any rate, it was a good thing they were gone. They might have been a problem, a lot of extra bodies in the way. It would have been a shame to have to kill so many innocent people. But it was going to be a delight to get these bastards that kept American grunts in chains, beating them with bamboo poles for amusement, pulling out their fingernails for playtime. Starvation, humiliation, torture. For six, nine, eleven years. That poor bastard Gougelmann. Beeker glanced at the house. It was hard to believe his friend was there.

Beeker thought of what it would be like to be a captive of one of these hateful groups. The men holding Gougelmann and the others were supposed to be Cambodians. Cambodians were just about the worst. As much as everyone bellyached about the actions of American troops and their Vietnamese enemies, the truth was they were the two most civilized groups participating in the war. The two least likely to act out of mere rage. Neither the Americans nor the VC had been thirsty for blood. At least not like the other groups involved. He remembered—

"No guards outside the bamboo," whispered Rosie directly behind him, interrupting his train of thought. That was good. It meant there were fewer Cambodians inside. Fine with him.

They crept closer and closer. The memories came back.

He remembered the way the VC would react with abject terror whenever they realized they were up against the South Koreans. No one frightened the VC the way the mere mention of the Koreans could. Those "brother Asians" had one point of view when it came to war: Kill everything that might conceivably kill back. This included, of course, old men, women, and even babies. Babies, after all, could grow up to be VC unless you pounded their brains out with the butt of your rifle. They recognized no civilian status, but slaughtered any human being that came before them. The Geneva rules had never been part of their operational strategy.

The Koreans were the most vicious and mean-hearted sons-of-bitches Beeker had ever seen. He recalled with disgust the way the Koreans would drag a Vietnamese woman out of her hooch in which her children were burning alive and not be content merely to rape her. They always made it a game to kill her at the same time, a slow-motion murder simultaneous with the gangbang. Each soldier would take a piece out of her with a knife when he was done using her. It was a long, painful waiting game to see how long she could be kept alive.

If all the bleeding hearts in the United States thought it was so terrible what American boys became after a stint in Nam, they should have wondered who changed them. Who was it that taught the peach-faced boys from Georgia and Colorado and Vermont how to be very effective killers?

It was the Australians with their far superior knowledge of the ways of Asians who taught the American greenhorns just how to enrage and terrify a population that seemed imperturbable and placid. It was simple. The Vietnamese to a man believe in reincarnation. Even the Catholics. Their vision of the next life said you arrived there in your own body. So the Australians always made sure the VC went on to their afterlife with some slight impairments.

Without ears, so they couldn't hear. Without tongues, so they couldn't speak. Without their peckers—to spend eternity eternally frustrated. At first the Americans couldn't face things like that. Why deface the dead? The Australians had a simple answer to that: it terrified the ones who were left alive. If that logic hadn't been persuasive, you didn't have to see more than two or three of your best friends murdered in an alien jungle before you discarded the amenities.

Soon these twenty-year-old American boys from Georgia, and Colorado, and Vermont, were wearing necklaces of human ears when they marched back into their own camps. If you wanted to convince a vacillating village that collaborating with the enemy wasn't such a hot idea, then you found a couple of VC and dropped their still-bleeding heads on the doorstep of the headman's hooch. He always got the message.

And the Cambodians. Everybody knew what the Cambodians could do. Or if they hadn't known it during Vietnam, they learned it soon afterward. To put it bluntly, the Cambodians had destroyed their own civilization. In three years, two thousand years of civilized life and culture had left to it nothing but pyramids of skulls that littered the countryside. Mere literacy was worth a death sentence to the revolutionaries. Not more than three doctors survived in a country with a population of five million. And it was Cambodians who held Gougelmann. After nine years Beeker wasn't sure that Gougelmann would want to be brought back. He might just want to be released with a bullet to his temple.

Beeker and Rosie got to their position. The sun was much brighter, even in this short time. It beat down upon them, and the inevitable stench of their bodies rose up to assault their noses. They waited silently, only occasionally glancing at their watches to gauge their own and the others' progress. Beeker realized in those last moments of waiting that this was the natural state of his life, his body, and his mind. The rancid sweat, the weight of the M16, the smells of the jungle, and the waiting, always the endless waiting at peak, was what he had been born for. All the clean showers and rich schoolboys and wives and television sets in the world were suddenly total bullshit, absolute bullshit. They were, he knew, the dream. They were the fantasy that he had sometimes mistaken for living. This was his reality.

If in the next five minutes he were to die, he would not regret having done what he did. He had got the team together once more. It would prove, he knew, a deadly reunion. At least for the Cambodians inside the French plantation house, but maybe even for himself and his friends. He glanced back at Rosie. The black man seemed to know what he was thinking. Rosie lifted one corner of his mouth. It wasn't even a whole smile. But it meant that Rosie agreed, that getting back together again was worth any price. They all felt that way. Beeker knew it.

That was what he was thinking when the thud of Cowboy's 16 sounded way on the other side of the perimeter. Beeker and Rosie didn't even think. They were just moving, fast, crouched over, hurtling toward the bamboo fence that separated the tiny yard of the house from the trampled fields.

They had to get there and do their work before the Cambodians had a chance to kill their captives. Beeker and his men were here to save American lives. It was their job, their duty, at that moment it was their very reason for existence. If there were Cambodians standing between them and the rescue of those American lives, too bad, Charlie. You got in the way.

Beeker and Rosie got to the opening in the bamboo fence before anyone had a chance to close it against them. Their two rifles spat out their automatic fire in an anarchistic splattering. The barrels of the M16s sent quick and easy death to three men who stood in the doorway to a small hut. The bullets had cut through their bellies so cleanly that they appeared to be in surgery, but then they fell to the ground, and blood began oozing in pools beneath their corpses.

Beeker took in everything with the quick, trained eye of a combat soldier. There were only three huts beside the main house, an ancient stone building that seemed an incongruous part of France in this distinctly Asian landscape. Perhaps it had once been surrounded by a park, or a lawn, or gardens, but nothing was left of that. All its land had been given over to the poppies. Nothing was left but the compound-sized area immediately surrounding the building. Applebaum and Harry appeared on Beeker's right. They had stopped on the blind side of each of the other two hooches and sent deadly fire through them. A few groans when the echo of the firing died away showed that some of the bullets had found targets. Harry stopped the groans with a high-explosive round from the grenade launcher.

Beeker glanced at Rosie. Rosie nodded agreement: *Something was wrong.*

So few guards, and all the guards there were seemingly

unprepared. It didn't feel right, not for an encampment that held eighteen American prisoners.

Billy Leaps and Rosie took shelter behind the hut and studied the stone mansion. It was almost with relief that Beeker detected movement inside. Rosie didn't hesitate to send a round through the first-floor window where they had seen a shadow.

Applebaum and Harry moved quickly after they checked that everyone in the huts was dead. Now the danger was isolated in the Frenchie house. They spread apart and moved farther away from one another and from Rosie and Beeker.

The sharp crack of a rifle answering Rosie's came from the house. First it came from a second-story window. It worked like a starter's gun. Immediately there was fire from every single window in the mansion's facade, a flame of fire out of every portal. The bullets kicked up dirt from the firm ground where they impacted. Billy Leaps's adrenaline pumped furiously as he realized the odds he and his men faced. Four against ten. Ten if all the Cambodians were firing. But there might be others inside, others whose job it was to kill the Americans rather than allow them to be rescued.

The four of them moved to better shelter, Beeker and Rosie behind wooden outbuildings, Applebaum behind a pile of broken masonry near the bamboo fence, Harry crouching behind a square stone well off to one side. They never ceased to answer the guns in the house. The noise was incredible— the sudden chatter of the M16s and the unmistakable clatter of AK-47s, the communist weapon they had all learned to hate and to respect. Over it all, the rip of Applebaum's M60 ruled. The reciprocal fire became a vicious, deadly duet, one they had all heard for years and years in Vietnam. The two sets of rifles sent siren songs of death through the air.

Beeker and his men were the better marksmen. Thank God.

Billy Leaps saw one man tumble from the second story with an agonizing yell that foretold his quick departure from this world. He had been hit low in the belly—you could tell that because he pitched forward. If he had been hit in the head, he would have slammed backward, deeper into the room. Billy Leaps decided to aim for the belly from now on. When they fell out of the windows onto the ground, it made the accounting easier. It also frightened the others, to see their comrades plummet to the earth.

All the time they had spent in Louisiana relearning their craft with the rifles was paying off. Another body hurtled down from the second story, end over end. "Lucky," thought Beeker, "you're going to get to hear and talk and fuck in the afterworld." The man's body hit the packed earth with a *thwump*, like a belly flop that missed the water entirely.

The firing from the house was no longer overwhelming. The men moved quickly and surely around the compound. They never stayed in one place long enough for the enemy fire to pin them down. They screamed their war cries as they answered each volley from the building with a deadly accurate bullet of their own.

Beeker had counted ten enemy guns when the fight started. Two were gone. Fuck Martinsdale. If they had had Applebaum's explosives, the whole thing would have been over by now. But at least it was still in control. They had their skill. They had their lovers, the M16s that had gotten them through Nam in one piece.

The enemy was going to die. Beeker felt that now.

He even began to think about the eighteen prisoners. Where would they be held? In the house. Not on the upper floors: too many windows, too many staircases. They'd be kept in the basement, where it was close and dark and airless.

Two more windows were silenced. These were on the first floor. The bodies flung backward into the rooms.

Beeker was taking aim at a man in dark green in one of the upstairs windows when quite suddenly the man's neck exploded. In an instant Beeker knew that the man had been shot from behind. The man's eyes were open wide, just like his mouth. Then he pitched forward and performed a humiliating somersault through the air and landed so that his spine snapped, and he was just a little huddle of blood and green cloth on the ground below. If he had been shot from behind, then one of them was in the house—and that had to be Cowboy. Everybody else was accounted for.

"First floor," Beeker yelled to Rosie. If Cowboy was upstairs, he could take care of things. They'd get the downstairs.

18

Cowboy's three-round burst to start the dance had been quickly identified by the guards in the house as a diversion. They had left only two men on the back of the house to deal with Cowboy. Cowboy had grinned to himself. He picked off one, and then exchanged fire with the other for about fifteen seconds. Then he simply stood out from behind the tree where he had been hidden, raised his M16, and fired directly into his opponent's face. The man got off one shot. Then his face exploded. The shot went wide of Cowboy, whose feeling was that a man not really trained for ground combat had to take a few chances. It served to equalize things.

For several seconds he debated what to do. The noise from the other side of the house was tremendous, but it was all somehow muffled by the stone bulkiness of the mansion. There was no more fire from the back. He could creep around the perimeter, behind the bamboo fence, and get to Harry and Applebaum's position. Or he could do the more dangerous thing.

He decided on that. Hell, if he was going to die, he might as well die having done the right thing.

He fired five shots at the back of the house. None of his fire was returned.

He ran directly up to the rear facade. The doors and windows of the first floor were all boarded over, some of them actually sealed with masonry. But there were mature vines growing up one corner, and slinging his M16 over his shoulder, Cowboy hoisted himself up the vines and climbed to the second floor. Most of the panes in the window there had already been broken out. Holding on to the vine, which was beginning to pull away from the building on account of his weight, he kicked at the frame of the window till it gave way. Then he slid into the room, just as the vine's suckers came loose from the building above his head and drooped heavily toward the ground.

The room in which Cowboy found himself had been a bedroom. It was nearly bare now, with just some sticks of broken-up furniture. The opulent wallpaper showed rainwater stains from above and urine stains nearer the floor. The parqueted flooring was heavily warped. There was a stink of garbage and feces there.

The door to the hallway was open, and the house was filled with the echo of the AK-47s. Cowboy crept to the hallway and peered out. A long passageway with a multitude of doors on either side. All the guards evidently were in the rooms that looked out to the front of the house, where Cowboy's buddies were.

He went directly across the hall, kicked open the door, and put a bullet through the back of the guard's neck. He tumbled out.

"A piece of cake," Cowboy murmured to himself with a grin.

He slipped back out into the hallway. The next doorway was open. He peered in. Two guards here, at adjoining windows, with great piles of ammunition between them. All the rooms were wrecked and bare and contained nothing but ammunition, the guards' flat pallets for sleeping, and piles of rotting garbage. God, but these men were pigs, thought Cowboy as he slaughtered one.

Right through the heart. He fell forward and was caught by the window ledge. The second man, hearing the report of the M16, turned with his rifle. And kept turning. Because his head exploded, the top of it anyway. Spraying Cowboy with blood and brains. "Thanks, Harry," said Cowboy, not knowing how he knew it was the Greek who had fired the shot. But he did know it. The triggered AK-47 fired madly into the parqueted floor, and then the corpse fell on top of it, staying there for a second with the barrel against the ground, like a weary laborer resting on his hoe.

Cowboy ran low past the great staircase to the other wing of the house. There had been two more in the first room, but one of them was already dead. Then his friend joined him. Cowboy always aimed for the neck. He didn't know why. Just habit, he guessed.

The last room had just one man. Those Cambodians might be pigs, but they certainly had a taste for symmetry. So did Cowboy. He pushed open the door and took aim at the back of the head of the man who was firing out the window.

He wasn't quiet enough. The man heard him. He turned. Cowboy was already squeezing the trigger.

"Cowboy," the target said. "You bastard—"

Cowboy fired.

Beeker noted that the entire second floor had been silenced. Two men remained on the first floor. It was easy now.

Rosie got one. Harry got one.

The dead men were draped over the windowsills like laundry hung out in the sun to dry. The dead men were huddled on the ground like bundles of stained rags waiting to be picked up by the junkman.

It was utterly quiet. No sound came from the house. Beeker held up his hand and signaled a cease-fire to the others.

Rosie suddenly appeared at his side.

"Those weren't Cambodians," he said. "Those were Kha."

The Kha were mountain tribesmen of Indochina, recruited and trained by the CIA. By natural bent they had become the best indigenous fighters of the war. There wasn't an American soldier in the war who had not respected the Kha.

"Beeker!"

It was Cowboy's voice, and it came from one of the upstairs windows.

"Cowboy!"

"Last room on the left. Upstairs," yelled Cowboy. He did not appear at the window. He didn't want to take any chance of being shot at by his buddies. "Get up here! Quick!"

"Position secured?" Beeker called. He wasn't taking any chances either.

"Position secured! Hurry, goddamn it!"

Cowboy had jerked the rifle at the last moment. He didn't get the last Kha tribesman in the neck. He got him in the chest. But the bullet still did the trick. The man died.

Beeker got inside the house and up the stairs. He found the room at the end. Cowboy was leaning against the wall, staring down at the corpse.

Cowboy shrugged. "It doesn't matter. He's dead."

Beeker was puzzled. He went over and peered down into the dead man's face.

"Cao Dinh!" he exclaimed.

Rosie came into the room as well. He looked at the dead man too.

"Tol' you they was Kha. Goddamn it, goddamn Kha." He

banged his rifle butt on the floor in his frustrated anger. Cao Dinh had led the indigenous forces that Beeker and his men had worked with in SOG, the Special Operations Group. He was a good soldier, a good man.

"Cao Dinh was holding our people prisoner?" demanded Billy Leaps of Cowboy. "I can't believe that. Not Cao Dinh. He was—"

"There aren't any fucking prisoners, Beeker," said Cowboy in disgust.

Beeker pulled back suddenly. Applebaum and Harry came into the room. Their laughter of triumphal glee was suddenly broken off when they heard Cowboy's last statement.

After a moment of shock, Beeker recovered himself. "No prisoners," he repeated. It was beginning to make sense. Not much, but more than before. They had just killed sixteen, seventeen brave men—men who had been their friends and allies in the war—in order to liberate eighteen American prisoners who didn't exist.

"When I saw it was Cao Dinh," said Cowboy, "I tried to pull my shot. Didn't work." His voice was harsh, almost choked.

"Did he say anything to you?"

"Yeah," said Cowboy bitterly, "he called me a bastard. And he said something else too."

"What?"

"He said there weren't any prisoners. And one more thing." Cowboy paused and looked around at his friends. "He said just one more thing before he fucking died."

"What did he say?" demanded Rosie, shaking in his anger.

"Just one word," said Cowboy. "*Parkes.*"

19

"Let's check it out," said Billy Leaps soberly. The five men turned away from the corpse that until a few minutes ago had harbored the soul of their friend. Harry squeezed Cowboy's shoulder once. Nobody blamed Cowboy for killing Cao Dinh. Any one of them would have got that shot off. Nobody had been asking for IDs that morning.

But how had it come about that they had murdered Cao Dinh and his men? Who had made that inevitable?

They went through the mansion systematically. Cowboy and Harry took the upper floor. Rosie and Billy Leaps scoured the lower. Applebaum checked around outside to make sure they had missed nothing.

There was no sign of life, none at all. Just corpses, just so much meat. Blood seeped out from bullet holes in each of them. Some wounds were clean, shots that had landed directly in the heart. Most had multiple wounds. One man's arm was barely still attached to his body. Another's lungs dragged in the dirt two feet below him as he hung over the first floor windowsill.

They found no sign that the place had ever been inhabited

by Americans. There were no indications that anyone had been held prisoner there. Most of the larger rooms on the first floor, it was apparent, had been used to house the workers. At any rate, that's the way they smelled.

They looked for carvings in the wooden walls, marks on the floor. They knew any American caught by the enemy would try to leave a trail for potential rescuers. Even after ten years they would have done that. At least Gougelmann would have. Billy Leaps knew in his bones that Gougelmann had never been inside this house.

The sun was blistering. The corpses on the sunny side of the house were beginning to stink and turn black in the heat. Billy Leaps hated the sight of the bodies; he hated the buzz of the flies lapping up the coagulating blood, not because he feared death, but because these deaths had been pointless.

Billy Leaps felt anger surge through him. He had ignored all his instincts and had trusted Parkes. He had been trapped by his desire to help out a fellow American who he thought had fallen prisoner of war. Parkes had got him good, got him in the one place he had known Beeker was vulnerable, his never-ending loyalty to his fellow warriors. It had led him to Laos, halfway round the world. For what? To slaughter eighteen innocent men, twelve in the house, six outside. To kill a headman of the Kha tribe who had fought beside Beeker in battle. Cao Dinh had led his brave mountain men in raid after raid that devastated the hope of the NVN that they might ever control this country.

Billy Leaps had no doubt that Parkes was behind this fiasco. Except that Billy Leaps knew it wasn't a fiasco for Parkes. They had done exactly what Parkes wanted them to do. They had killed off everybody in the house. But why? Why? That was what was still unclear to Billy Leaps.

Beeker looked blankly at Rosie and realized that he had

betrayed this man. And Cowboy, Applebaum, and the Greek. He had ignored his grandmother's most stringent warning by using the overwhelming skill of the team to wreak evil.

He damned his warrior soul for its ability to become a tool for evil as well as good. He was a machine, a fighting machine just the way the Marines had told him he was in boot camp. He remembered the endless repetitions. *I am a United States Marine. I am a fighting machine.* He had been trained to that. The training had stuck. He was a fighting machine today, at the age of thirty-seven, one of the deadliest killers in the world. And a killer not always able to discern in what direction to turn those horrible, those terrible, those awesome skills. He had trained his body; he had trained his mind, and the bodies and the minds of his men—but he had forgot to train their souls. How could he have allowed Parkes to maneuver them into this?

Rosie seemed, as always, to divine his thoughts. They stood in the middle of an empty room. It stank of old habitation, but not the presence of Americans. "We had to do it, Beeker," he said. "We didn't do it for Gougelmann, man, we did it for us."

Rosie was right, of course. He put his finger on it. Billy Leaps had never really believed that Gougelmann was still alive. None of the other men had either. Gougelmann was dead and rotting in his San Diego grave. But that hadn't mattered. What had mattered was getting the team together again. He realized now that any excuse would have done.

Beeker smiled a grim smile. He caught a sudden glimpse of the future.

His reverie was broken by the sound of running footsteps. Cowboy and Applebaum burst into the room. "We have company," Cowboy said.

"Looks like Americans. At least they're white," added Applebaum.

"How many?" Beeker asked,

"Half dozen," said Cowboy. "Coming up the road like they own the place. In Jeeps, old ones, looks like they're from the war."

Harry walked in then. "I was doing a patrol," he said, certain the other two would have made the most important announcement. "They look strange out here. Like civilians."

Beeker thought quickly. "Cover me. I'm going to be the greeting party."

Cowboy protested: "Billy Leaps, don't be a fool. There's no such thing as a greeting party in this part of the world. Let's just set up an ambush—"

"No. I'm going to meet them. I want to know who they are and what they want." He looked at each of his men in turn, catching every man's eye for a brief second. "I have a pretty good idea who sent them. Now I want to know what they're after. I'm going to find out why we were brought here." There was no argument. The team knew their leader was right. "Spread out around the building. See anything funny happening, shoot first, don't wait for them to answer any questions."

That order was superfluous, Billy Leaps knew. His men were trained. Sometimes he thought with pride that he could command this group even if he were as mute as the boy he had left at home.

Billy Leaps strode to the front door of the house. He stood in the wide entrance, with the bullet-torn doors thrown open on either side of him. His men had scattered through the building. They stood out of sight at windows, using the Kha corpses for cover. They breathed through their mouths to avoid the gathering stink of Asian death.

Beeker came down to the lowest of the stone steps so that his men might see him and any signal he chose to give. His legs were spread wide, his arms held his rifle at his chest, his face was set with grim determination. In some private way this was his act of repentance to his men. After his overwhelming sense of responsibility for having brought them back to Indochina on a false mission and having exposed them to such danger, he would now stand alone to face a probable enemy. He would be the one to receive the first fire. He would take the first wave of any heat. Not them. Him, alone. Their leader.

The sound of the Jeeps became louder. They were coming directly into the compound. Billy Leaps's hands tightened on his rifle. The cartridge was loaded. There were thirty deadly rounds of ammunition in his hands, more hanging at his belt, ready to be put into the M16 at a moment's notice.

The nose of the first Jeep pushed through the narrow entry, dredging up a short section of the bamboo fence. Two more followed. Two men in each of the three vehicles, all of them white. All of them American. All of them CIA. They had the look, wore the clothes, and carried the attitude. They stank of the Agency like the Kha corpses stank of death.

The Jeeps stopped. The men climbed out of the vehicles with broad smiles. The one who was obviously in charge walked forward to the stone steps in front of the house, the steps that were chipped and gouged by bullets.

"Billy Leaps Beeker, right?" The toothpaste teeth grinned at the Cherokee. "Had your picture of course. Knew it'd be you. Would have known anyway. You half-breeds are all alike. Easy-going bright eyes, but under there somewhere, a real vicious son-of-a-bitch." The man thought he was making a good-humored joke with a buddy, someone who'd laugh with him. He was the sort of man who'd call Rosie "one bad-ass nigger" to his face. Billy Leaps didn't laugh. No one joked about his father's legacy and the Cherokee blood that flowed in his veins. Correction: no one joked that way and lived.

The man's hand was brought forward. It waved there in midair. Billy Leaps made no motion to let go of his rifle.

The agent pretended not to be embarrassed. He looked around the compound, taking in the sight of the dead Kha bodies. "You really did it, didn't you, Beeker? Sure as hell did." This acted as a kind of signal for the others to begin to walk around the compound, as if to study the corpses. But the ploy to surround Billy Leaps was obvious.

"Why are you here?" asked Billy Leaps calmly. He didn't bother asking who they were or who had sent them. Both answers were obvious, and Billy Leaps did not care to hear what lies they chose to proffer.

The leader turned his head sharply at the command in Billy Leaps's voice. The casualness he put into his reply was an effort. "Checking on your work, that's all. But we knew you'd do a good job. You and your men."

With this he looked around, as if expecting Beeker's men to come out of hiding. They did not. And Beeker did not make the mistake of glancing back at the house, giving away their position.

"Why didn't you help?"

"You didn't need any help," said the CIA leader amiably, glancing around at the corpse-strewn yard. "You're the soldiers. We're just civilians."

"But you were close enough to hear the firing?" Beeker asked.

The agent smiled. "And when the firing stopped."

"My men are dead because of you," said Beeker savagely. "I lost my whole team because you didn't fucking come to help. Why do you show up now? That's what I want to know."

"All your men dead?" His smile didn't fade, but something about his whole attitude changed perceptibly. He was no longer conciliatory; he was menacing. "I'm very sorry about that. They were good men. I've seen their records. They died in a good cause, let me assure you. Now, we have to get inside the house and secure the documents we came for."

"Documents?"

"Documents vital to national security."

A CIA man died with a lie on his lips. Always. He never remembered what it was to tell the truth.

All six agents moved toward the front entrance of the house.

Beeker raised his rifle. "You don't take anything out of this compound, not until you explain about Gougelmann and the seventeen other American POWs. Who don't exist. And why the guards on this place weren't Cambodians, but Kha." The six agents moved a couple of steps closer. "If anybody moves one step closer, he's a dead man." It didn't sound like a threat, just a statement of fact.

"You're being difficult about this, Mr. Beeker." The man's smile persisted, the way some smells do, even after the shit has been shoveled out.

The agents' hands went inside their tropical suits, and each one of them pulled out a pistol. Or started to.

Thank you, Billy Leaps said silently, *thank you for the excuse.*

Without giving any indication that he was preparing for it, without a single one of his muscles prematurely tensing, Billy Leaps dove to the left. With complete control of his M16 he sent a murderous burst of bullets into the air. Even though he was in motion, the tumbling .223s hit their target. They sliced through the brow of the CIA leader as though they were an invisible knife cutting through bone. Waves of red blood and gray brain cells were tossed through the air.

The suits of the two men nearest their leader were ruined. But it didn't matter to them. Nothing else ever would, either. Because even as Billy Leaps's M16 was firing, death was shooting out of four windows of the house as well. The five white-suited men never realized where the bullets were coming from. They collapsed like pins at a bowling alley, except that pins at a bowling alley don't twitch and bleed.

It was over in seconds. The guns were silenced. Then Billy Leaps jumped up, unharmed. Of the six agents trained by the CIA, one had managed to fire his pistol. One bullet, straight into the earth. His own blood filled up the hole it made.

Beeker's men shouted victory from the windows. Billy Leaps motioned them down. He went through the bodies. Two of them lived.

Billy Leaps pointed them out to Rosie. "Can you keep those two going till we talk to them?"

The black medic worked on one of the men. "Do him a favor, Beeker" was all he said, rising from the ground.

Beeker knew what Rosie meant. In Nam they had all heard the desperate cries of wounded Americans on the field. Men trapped beyond the reach or the help of medics. Men begging to be allowed to die. They were bleeding to death. Their legs had been chopped off, their genitals sliced out, shrapnel had popped their eyeballs like cream-filled chocolates. Beeker remembered.

Without emotion or thought, Beeker walked up to the agent on the ground. He trusted Rosie's prognosis. Rosie the medic had seen more death come slowly and with agony than anyone else Beeker knew. He put the barrel of his rifle at the forehead of the wounded man. Billy Leaps looked into the dying man's eyes and pulled the trigger. That one bullet saved the man a lot of pain.

Rosie ignored the sound of the rifle shot. The others hadn't watched. Beeker had done what was necessary according to their ethic. That was all. If the others thought about it, it was only to say, *He'd do the same for me . . .*

"This one's gonna make it easy!" cried Rosie, delighted. "Just a couple of clean shots through the shoulder and thigh. Clean as a whistle. He'll be sore for a couple of months. Bones, organs, arteries all okay. One lucky bastard, this guy."

"We're out of practice," murmured Applebaum apologetically.

From his pack Rosie brought out antiseptics and bandages. He filled a syringe and shot the man with morphine. "He's gonna be just fine."

20

Rosie worked his magic, with alcohol and stitches and bandages. The man's eyes opened an hour later, glazed with the effect of the morphine. He was young, about twenty-eight, Beeker imagined. Probably he'd been the youngest of the group of six. That didn't change the fact that he was Agency all the way. He already had the clothes and the act down perfectly.

They had taken him into the wide marble-floored foyer of the stone mansion and closed the front door against the heat and the bright sunlight. It was nearly eleven o'clock in the morning.

He looked around him vaguely for a short while, and then his panic took over from the drug. His adrenaline gave him a sudden alertness.

"How long have I been out?" he demanded. Only Rosie and Beeker were there to hear him. The rest had gone back on guard.

So far as Beeker was concerned, this was a hostile prisoner. He would use the rules that applied to that situation. The start was simple: you never let a prisoner know anything concrete about his situation. Keep him in suspense. Keep him guessing. Beeker and Rosie were silent.

The man made a garbled and ridiculous attempt to stand. The movement activated his sense of pain beyond the morphine's ability to control it. He collapsed back onto the floor.

"What's your hurry?" asked Rosie.

"Am I going to die?" the young man asked. His skin was darkly tanned from the oriental sun. His brown hair had the waves of a college student. His clean-shaven face was smooth and unblemished. Beeker imagined him the Big Man on Campus at some state university in the Midwest.

Keep the prisoner in suspense. There was no reason for him to know his wounds weren't serious. His body was half-covered in bandages. Some blood had seeped through and stained the whiteness. It looked bad, especially to someone who wasn't used to the sight of battle injuries. Let him wonder just how bad off he was.

"Look," the young man cried, grabbing Rosie's powerful forearm, "you got to tell me."

Rosie pulled away.

"What's your name?" said Beeker.

"Holladay," the young man answered automatically. "Where are the others?"

"Dead," said Beeker.

"All of them?" whispered Holladay. Beeker remembered what it had been like that first time, to hear that five guys you knew were all dead, all at once, and you were the only survivor.

"Why did you and your dead friends come here?" asked Beeker. "What were you after?"

"Documents."

"Bullshit," said Rosie in a low voice. He was sitting against the scarred wainscoted wall, cleaning his rifle.

"Bullshit," echoed Billy Leaps.

Holladay blinked. Tears came to his eyes. Tears of pain, and of fear.

"Let me tell you something," said Billy Leaps. "You're a lucky bastard. There's no good reason why you should be alive. I got one of my men who's upset because you didn't die out there in the courtyard. He's upset because somebody's aim was off. If you don't talk to me, I'm just gonna turn you over to him."

Rosie chuckled. "Applebaum'd love that. Applebaum would love to rectify his error in lettin' you live, white meat. He wouldn't just shoot you, neither. He's our plastiques man. Plastiques-Man to the rescue!"

Billy Leaps saw the terror in Holladay's eyes. "If I tell you," he stammered, "will you get me out of here? Will you get me over to Thailand to a hospital?"

"The only thing I'm going to promise," said Beeker, "is that you'll get more morphine."

That was enough. Holladay obviously thought he was dying. And if he was dying, what did it matter what he said? He was vulnerable. His superior officer—the only one he had ever answered to—was dead. There was no one left to judge him.

"There aren't any documents," he said to Beeker.

Rosie continued to clean his M16, but he was listening intently. You could tell by his expression.

"What were you coming to get then?" said Billy Leaps.

"I don't know. Something else. I wasn't told. But money, I think."

"Money!" exclaimed Rosie.

"From the poppies, right?" said Beeker. It was all beginning to make more sense.

"I guess," said Holladay, and he winced with pain.

Beeker motioned Rosie over. Rosie fished in his bag and prepared another shot of morphine. He administered it while Beeker and Holladay continued their exchange.

"So this whole fucking operation was to raid a fucking *safe*?" said Billy Leaps angrily.

"No," said Holladay. "It was to get rid of Cao Dinh and his men too."

"Why?"

"I don't know." Holladay paused. Not knowing was the old way. It was what the Agency demanded. If you're not told about something directly, you don't know anything about it. If you figured something out, you kept it to yourself. "Cao Dinh was one of ours, I'm pretty sure."

"For the last twenty years he was," said Billy Leaps sarcastically. "And he was running this operation here for the Agency, right?"

"I . . . I don't know," said Holladay. "I don't work for the Agency."

Billy Leaps blinked. "You're trying to tell me—"

"We work for Prometheus," Holladay said with pride, foolish, foolish pride. It was as ridiculous and out of place as the stuff that Applebaum pulled sometimes. "We're more elite than the Agency."

"We're working for Prometheus too," said Beeker bitterly. "And if we're working for Prometheus, and you were working for Prometheus, and Cao Dinh and his men were working for Prometheus, then why are there so many corpses?"

"Cao Dinh was a traitor," said Holladay complacently.

Billy Leaps nearly shot the man right then and there. For his stupidity, in believing everything that had been told to him by his superiors. Then Beeker realized that there might be a good deal more to be got out of this man. *Elite*, garbage. Holladay was as dumb as anybody the CIA had ever recruited. "Cao Dinh was a traitor to Prometheus, you mean?"

Holladay nodded slowly. "So it was your job to come in and get him."

"And then it was your job to come in and get *us*," said Rosie, who had resumed his work with the rifle.

"No," said Holladay, who had grown almost chatty with the morphine. "We had a two-prong mission. The first imperative was to retrieve the money. It must have been money; I can't think of anything else it would be. What sort of documents would they keep around *here*? And the second thing we were supposed to do was see how well you guys did. Hey, you guys did great! You got eighteen men—"

"You knew exactly how many men Cao Dinh had here?"

"Sure. You got all Cao Dinh's men without sustaining a single injury."

"Applebaum scraped his knee," said Rosie. "I put Mercurochrome on it. Man nearly cried."

"See," said Holladay, "this was a kind of training mission for you. And if you did all right, then Mr. Parkes was going to use you again. He figured once you got back in business you couldn't stop."

"And if we didn't do all right? If some of us had gotten ourselves killed?"

Holladay was silent. He didn't have to speak. Beeker knew the answer. If the team had proved unworthy, then Holladay's group had instructions to finish them off. For a few moments Billy Leaps felt sorry for this kid. He might be twenty-eight, but he was still a kid. He still didn't understand. Parkes had set up two groups: the six CIA men, and Beeker and his group. Parkes, that bastard, was testing both. If Beeker and his men had failed against the Kha, they weren't worth much anyway. The "civilian" group had leave to finish them off. If they won against the Kha, they still had to stand up against his six agents in their immaculate tropical whites, exercising their shoulder pistols and their subtle brains. Parkes didn't care who won. If Holladay's people had overcome Beeker and his men by stealth, then Parkes would have kept them on, to trounce other opponents by stealth. As it was, Beeker and his team had beaten both Cao Dinh and the civilians. They had passed Parkes's test with flying colors. Only trouble was, twenty-three men were dead.

Holladay thought he had just been unlucky. He still didn't understand that he had been set up by the head of Prometheus. Probably he wouldn't have believed Beeker if Beeker had explained Parkes's elaborate double cross. No man as dumb as Holladay could ever be brought to think of himself as expendable.

Billy Leaps knew there probably wasn't much more to be got out of Holladay directly, but he wanted him to continue to talk.

"What were you told about us?"

"Everything," said Holladay. "Full dossiers. You're their top team." Billy Leaps and Rosie exchanged glances, but Holladay couldn't see that. "But we had some concerns." Holladay talked as if he had been going to strategy meetings with Parkes twice a week. "See, your records weren't totally erased. They had to take care of that. I mean, there wasn't any record in the normal files about what you did in Vietnam. The high command had already sheep-dipped you. But there were traces, here and there. In the Pentagon. Some veterans' stuff slipped through. I took care of some of that. And now you're all dead. You never fought in Vietnam, and you never served in the United States military. See, Mr. Parkes was getting everything ready—"

"Ready for what?" asked Rosie casually.

"Ready to use you," said Holladay. "What else? Then when we discovered the terrorist group—"

"What terrorist group?" Beeker demanded.

"The Kha," Holladay said, with labored exasperation. "Those guys you just killed. Cao Dinh and his people." Holladay actually believed the idiotic words he had just spoken. Hadn't the man figured it out yet?

It was easy, thought Billy Leaps. Cao Dinh had been running a poppy farm for Parkes. Whether Parkes got the money himself—he had always been a greedy bastard—or whether it was funneled back up to the Agency like in the glory days of Air America, Beeker had no idea and no opinion. But that was the story. And Cao Dinh had severed ties with Parkes, maybe because of an argument, maybe because Parkes got too greedy, maybe because Cao Dinh had decided to throw his allegiance elsewhere. And so Parkes had sent in Beeker and his men to wipe out Cao Dinh and his Kha guards. The poppy farm would have been turned over to someone more trustworthy. That was the story.

"Prometheus couldn't do it. Or anybody else, for that matter. But you guys were ready by then. You were all set. So Mr. Parkes activated you. That's why you're here. Don't you understand?"

"I understand," said Billy Leaps. "Mr. Parkes wanted us to take care of Cao Dinh's terrorist army."

"All eighteen of 'em," said Rosie.

"He was something, that one," said Holladay, as if with reluctant admiration. "He was capable of upsetting the whole balance of power in the southeast sector of Asia. No doubt about it," said Holladay, obviously parroting a superior's words, "Cao Dinh could have initiated—"

"A domino effect!" cried Rosie gleefully.

Holladay turned his head painfully. "That's it. That's it exactly. So he had to be stopped."

Beeker rose from the floor. "Watch him, Rosie," he said. He walked down the first floor hallway and found a room without a corpse. He went inside, shut the door, leaned against the wall, and thought.

Their situation was not enviable. They were in Laos, a

country with whom the United States had very few relations at all. They were there illegally. They were holed up in a house with twenty-three dead men and a wounded CIA agent. Correction: Prometheus agent. Their ammunition was limited, as was their food. The Mekong River border was twenty-three miles away.

Two hours ago they had fought a bloody battle with Kha tribesmen. The noise of that fight might have been heard in the surrounding countryside—in fact, it would be pretty damned strange if it hadn't been. Even with the limited communication facilities in this nation, news of that fight must have reached the nearest provincial capital. Troops, guards, soldiers, policemen— men with guns, at any rate—might be on their way.

With that decision made, he looked up and was about to leave the room to confer with his men. But his eye caught something. It was a standing chest in the corner of the room—the only piece of whole furniture he had seen in the house. This one was scarred, but it was intact. He went to the chest and pulled open the doors. It was empty.

He had an intuition.

He went to the door, opened it, and called down the corridor: "Applebaum! Applebaum! Get your ass in here!"

21

There had to be a basement to the house. Of course! All the Indo-chinese had learned long ago never to keep anything of value above ground. They had lived with bombs and grenades, mortars and shells, for decades of unending war. With the Japanese, then the French, with one another, then with the Americans.

Applebaum rushed in, pleased to be singled out for Beeker's command. Beeker pointed to the chest. The two men placed their rifles against the wall and then pushed the chest aside. Beneath was a trapdoor. Stairs led down into blackness.

"Get a flashlight," said Beeker.

"I found a kerosene lamp in the kitchen," said Applebaum. "That's better, isn't it?"

Beeker nodded, and Applebaum ran off happily. Billy Leaps waited. He didn't mind that. If anybody were alive below, it would give him time to get nervous. Presently Applebaum returned with the lighted lamp.

Beeker walked down the stairs carefully and slowly. He sensed movement. Applebaum was right behind him with the lamp held in his outstretched arm to cast as much light as possible.

The movement was rats. Beady red eyes stared back at them from the corner of the basement room.

The cellar was half as large as the house itself. Beeker and Applebaum checked closely to see if there was any sign of human life. None was there.

But there had been. A PRC-10 sat on a table on the far side of the room. A small arsenal of AK-47s and ammunition to match was stacked in another corner. It was a good thing that Cowboy got the Kha's flank and ended that fire fight. Cao Dinh's men could have held off the entire Thai army with that.

"Hot damn," said Applebaum, respect in his voice. "They had a whole crate of Claymores here. Fuckin' idiots could have blown us to kingdom come with that shit."

Beeker looked at the vicious explosives. "Must have been captured during the war. Maybe they didn't know how to use them. Maybe whoever did know how to use them wasn't around. Who knows? But you're right, I'm glad they stuck to their rifles. This stuff would have been trouble."

"Lots of trouble." Applebaum meant it. He might be the biggest asshole the other Black Berets had ever allowed to live, but he was also one of the most knowledgeable men in the world when it came to explosives. And he had gotten his knowledge under battlefield conditions, not in an abandoned rock quarry back in the States. Applebaum loved explosives, but only when he was controlling the aim and the detonation. Applebaum had a soft spot in his heart for Claymores, but not when they were on the other side.

"Stuff's been here awhile," said Beeker as Applebaum gently wiped off a layer of dust. "Still good?"

"Always good," said Marty.

"Probably been here for years. Probably they even forgot about them. Too bad for them. Good thing for us."

Beeker—always the commander thinking of the future—vowed he'd never overlook a resource this way. His men would never go into battle and be like those idiots who graduated from West Point—the ones who thought they knew everything because they had read the book. The ones who would forget they had a skilled marksman in their ranks or someone like Applebaum who managed to turn three sticks of dynamite tied with a piece of string into a weapon that was both subtle and sure. It was the thing a good commander did—to remember all his resources, to utilize all his men's skills. And to note the foolish mistakes of an enemy to make sure he didn't ever make them himself.

In a third corner of the room was an old desk of scarred gray metal. Beeker leaned over it. The desk was littered with papers bearing the curious Cambodian script.

Beeker emptied the drawers of the desk onto the floor. He found nothing but a few pens, a sheaf of blank paper, and several small bills of Laotian currency. Certainly nothing worth the CIA—or Prometheus—allowing twenty-three men to die for.

"Applebaum, hold the lamp where I can see something, goddamn it!"

Applebaum was standing several feet away from the desk, peering at another large chest. He had opened the doors already and found it contained nothing but more rounds of ammunition.

Applebaum and Beeker glanced at each other. There was no reason to keep rounds of ammunition in a chest. It wasn't even AK-47 ammo. Applebaum handed Beeker the lamp and began unloading the heavy cartridges from the chest, tossing them behind him. When the chest was empty, and therefore much lighter, he and Beeker pushed it out of the way.

Behind the chest was a small iron door set into the stone wall. It was bolted and locked several times.

"This is why I wanted you," said Beeker.

"You knew this would be here?"

"This, or something like it. Can you get in it?"

"Sure."

"But don't demolish it. I want whatever's inside. Just get the locks off. Maybe you could even just shoot them off."

"No, no way." Applebaum knew bullets wouldn't do the job. But something else would, and Applebaum grinned when he thought of it. "Beeker, there's no prob, no prob. We got the best thing possible right here. Those Claymores. I'll just take a little C-4 out of one, and I'll have the prettiest can opener you ever saw. It'll just melt away those hinges, open up that safe like it was Pandora's box."

"Fine, fine," said Beeker. "Just get on with it."

"No prob, Beeker. I am your man!" Applebaum ignored Billy Leaps's impatience, not just because he was so happy that his leader had called on his expertise, but also because he knew it wouldn't do to hurry with Claymores.

He went to the box and lifted the block of C-4 out of one of the antipersonnel mines. He brought it to the desk.

"Billy Leaps, hold the lamp for me, but for shit's sake, don't hold it too close. I don't know how stable this stuff is, and I'd hate to take us out this late in the game." Applebaum rarely used the Cherokee's nickname. Only when he was working with explosives, his specialty, did he feel fully a part of the team. But now he was in his element and proud of the work he was capable of.

With the look of a kid playing with modeling clay, Applebaum carved a chunk of the plastic explosive off the block and began rolling it into a thin ribbon. "What you're looking at, Mr. Beeker, is a 1.5-pound block of C-4 plastic explosive. This is 90 percent RDX, the most powerful explosive known to man out-side the nasty ol' nukes. In the M18A1 Claymore, detonation of this block will project 700 ball bearings over a 60-degree arc for a distance of 50 meters at a height of 1 to 2 meters. What you're looking at is the biggest, nastiest sawed-off shotgun on earth. And we got a bunch of them."

Applebaum was working as he spoke; he slid the ribbon of plastic into the cracks of the iron door, and then when he had surrounded the door, he slid a detonator from the crate into the fattest part of the ribbon. He laid out det cord across the room. While the skinny little guy had been finishing up his preparations, Beeker policed the room, moving the AKs and their ammunition to the other side of the room and knocking the desk over to give cover from the blast.

Applebaum moved behind the desk, the clacker for command detonation in his hand. "Go on up, sir. I'll stay down here." Billy Leaps didn't argue. He handed Applebaum the lamp and rushed up the stairs. He ran down the hallway to the foyer of the building. The Prometheus agent Holladay lay asleep on the cool marble floor, his head cushioned by a rolled jacket taken from one of the corpses. Rosie was keeping watch and looked up at Beeker in surprise.

A few moments later there was a short, sharp crack followed closely by an awesome clang. The floor shook with the violence of it.

"What the fuck—" cried Rosie, rising from the floor.

"It's all right," said Billy Leaps quickly. "It's just Applebaum, having a good time. Tell the others not to come in firing."

Beeker ran back. Black smoke billowed up out of the cellar, and rising up through the trapdoor, like a devil out of a smoking hell, was Applebaum, grinning wide with a soot-covered face.

"Am I your man or am I your man?"

They waited a few minutes for the smoke to clear, though this didn't take long. Down below, the hinges on the iron door had been destroyed and the door neatly blasted across the room.

"Holy shit," said Applebaum in a low voice.

No Asian trusted his country's paper money, and evidently Parkes hadn't either. Paper money was a commodity you spent as soon as you got it, or else turned it in for gold and jewels. Gold and jewels outlasted regimes and other men's lives. What was behind the iron door had outlasted the lives of Cao Dinh and his men.

Kilo and half-kilo ingots of gold were stacked along the floor of the shallow closet. Small wooden chests held gems, cut and uncut, sorted only according to type. There were little boxes of dusky rubies, a larger box of the indigenous emeralds, several boxes of faceted diamonds that looked as if they had been wrenched out of a thousand wedding rings of a thousand gold-digging whores.

"Oh, God," whispered Applebaum, "we're rich, Billy Leaps, we're fucking rolling in it."

"If we ever get out of here alive," Billy Leaps cautioned.

He knew now why Parkes was willing to sacrifice so many men. Not only to punish Cao Dinh for his rebellion, not only to determine which was his best team, but also to recover this mineral wealth. There was enough here in gold and jewels for Cao Dinh to have uprooted just about any Indochinese government he chose. Enough for Parkes to become wholly independent of CIA control, if he had any now. Enough for Beeker and his four men for the rest of their lives.

"Go out and look in those Jeeps, Applebaum. They must have brought something along to carry this stuff away in."

Applebaum raced up the stairs. Billy Leaps held up the lamp and studied the contents of the shallow closet. So much wealth represented in that small space. A lifetime of wealth for himself and his men.

Wealth brought care, however, just as poverty did. And the

care this wealth brought on was instantaneous. It seemed imperative now that Beeker get his men out. They had to go right back to Thailand. The idea for a quiet night in the compound was past. They'd have to march back through the jungle as soon as possible. They had a casualty—the agent Holladay—and now they had a fortune to protect as well. The idea of Laotian troops on their way seemed no longer just a vague possibility. If they had any idea of what had been secreted in this derelict house, they'd be coming on with every speed. The Laotians would do a lot for so much easily convertible wealth. Beeker and his men might be in very real danger.

Applebaum returned carrying half a dozen canvas bags. Beeker examined them quickly. They were sturdy and heavily lined—the leader of the group had evidently known what form his booty was to take. Beeker began to fill up the bags. He stuck in as many half-kilo ingots as he could in each of five sacks, then filled up the hollows with jewels. That distributed the weight evenly. When this was done, many ingots of gold remained, as well as some silver bars that he had come across in a dim corner.

"I want to take everything," said Applebaum.

"One bag for each of us," said Billy Leaps. "No point in being greedy about this." He grinned.

They hefted the five bags and carried them upstairs. But Applebaum, going first up the dark stairs, stooped and blocked Beeker's way.

"Go on," said Billy Leaps.

"Don't you hear it?" said Applebaum in a whisper. A frightened whisper.

Whoop-whoop.

Distant still, but unmistakable.

Helicopters.

22

"They're Hueys!" Cowboy shouted.

He and Harry had been on patrol outside and had rushed into the mansion to alert the others.

"How many?" demanded Beeker.

"Three," said Harry. "Coming on hard."

The all too familiar Cobras. The flying death machines of the war. "We must have abandoned dozens . . . hundreds when we left," said Cowboy in a low awed voice. He had been wishing for a Huey, wishing hard ever since he landed in Thailand. He had them now, three of them, but they were on the other side.

Beeker's men looked to him for direction.

The *whoop-whoop* was louder now.

"Hovering," said Cowboy. From their position inside the first floor hallway they could not see the copters, but Cowboy knew by the sound. The three Hueys were stalled in midair just in front of and above the mansion.

"Back against here," said Beeker, indicating two interior walls of the first floor corridor.

The five men flattened themselves. They were positioned so

that at least two walls separated them from the outside. Straight fire, even grenades, would not touch them. From where they stood, they could see no windows.

But they had forgotten Holladay.

"Great Christ!" said Rosie. "Holladay, you fuck!"

The agent, confused in mind, had heard the noise of the helicopters and had thought it was a Prometheus team come to rescue him. He pulled himself up off the floor and lurched to the front doors of the mansion. He pushed the double doors open and held his bandaged arms out wide in welcome.

The vast metal hummingbirds spewed forth destruction. They launched their grenades from the two 40mm launchers. Little blasts of flame from the barrels produced thundering explosions in the compound. The Prometheus Jeeps blew up, one by one. The bamboo fences fell apart like toothpicks. The wooden hooches burst into flame.

Holladay, riddled with shrapnel from the frag grenades, staggered backward, blood spurting from a dozen deep wounds. He fell backward, and his head cracked loudly on the marble floor.

"They're gonna incinerate us," said Harry. His voice was calm.

"No," said Billy Leaps. "They're not going to firebomb the house." Beeker knew—or at least he goddamned well hoped—that the Laotians had their orders not to destroy the structure.

The three machines sending their echoing *whoop-whoop* through the jungle air moved in more closely to the target. They opened up with their powerful machine guns, sending hundreds of rounds of deadly ammunition flying through the air to eat up the human flesh of the corpses that still hung from the windows. Beeker wondered if it didn't look as though some of the Kha corpses were trying to defend themselves from the windows. The helicopter pilots couldn't have heard small arms fire. They wouldn't have known for sure that the Kha were dead, and they certainly weren't going to guess.

The bombardment lasted five minutes. There must have been enough metal in the compound now to outweigh all the dead twice over. Finally satisfied, the three helicopters left off their firing and pulled back, as if better to survey their handiwork.

Billy Leaps went cautiously into one of the front rooms, eased up to a window, and peered out. It was just as he thought. Everything in the compound itself that would burn was on fire, but those small conflagrations would die out quickly. The machine gun fire against the house had been so heavy that the Kha guard in the window had been completely cut in half. His shoulders, arms, and head had fallen outside the window onto the ground. His lower torso and legs had slipped back onto the room's parquet floor.

The helicopters set down a hundred yards away in the poppy fields.

Billy Leaps rushed back to his men. "Out the back, quick, quick. And everybody take one of those bags." He indicated the canvas sacks that he and Applebaum had dragged up from the cellar.

Cowboy said, "Everything's boarded up on the first floor." He pointed upstairs. Each carrying his pack, his rifle, and one fifth of the captured treasure, the men rushed up the stairs. They entered one of the rooms at the back of the house and without hesitation went to the windows and dropped the fifteen feet to the ground.

Crouching low, they ran to the bamboo fence in the back, still intact, and in five minutes more were hidden in the forest.

They went back through the jungle. They moved with speed no one would have thought possible. The sight of the bombardment propelled them, in part. And the thought of all the gold and gems they were carrying pulled them on. It was a fortune, a goddamn fortune in those five bags. A fortune to last the rest of their lives.

Each man dreamed of what he would do. Beeker had already said that once the fortune was turned into cash it would be divided five ways. Five equal ways.

Harry tried hard to come up with a fantasy of what to do with the money, so much money none of them could even begin to calculate it. He envisioned a bigger, brighter Harry's Bar in Chicago. A better neighborhood, a better clientele. A clientele that wouldn't call him "a hairy-assed Greek." That seemed dull and boring. He thought of a bungalow in Palm Springs. Then what the hell was he supposed to do all day, watch fucking television?

Applebaum's vision was brighter. *I'm going back to Vegas and blow the whole wad. I'll break the fucking bank in every fucking casino. And I'll have so many girls hanging on me. I'll have to brush their tits out of my face to see the goddamn roulette wheel.* But after that? Applebaum was stymied.

Rosie was going to take a thousand dollars in cash, one-dollar bills, and throw it out the window. That was it. That was all he could think of. What did he need money for? There wasn't a major medical center in the United States that wouldn't pay him top dollar for his specialty. There weren't more than half a dozen good skinners in the whole country. And the other five were drunks. He could get all the money he ever needed when he went back. The loot from Laos was just that—loot.

Bankroll a new plane, thought Cowboy. *Then start up the run to South America again. And goddamn kill any double cross-ers. A jet this time.* But something was wrong. He didn't feel the excitement. Maybe it was just that he had lost the craving for cocaine. Goddamn it, that was life. Now that he could afford it, he didn't care whether he got it or not.

Billy Leaps would buy land, a parcel to the northeast that

had recently come on the market. Tear down his neighbor's house and let the forest take over those goddamn soybean fields. A new pickup. And teach the boy how to shoot, just woodchuck; all the kid had to know was how to shoot woodchuck. But that didn't take any money, Billy Leaps realized with a start. He got a new pickup every couple of years anyway. And shells for the hunting rifles; that wasn't what you'd call a major expense.

Even in this first flush of newfound wealth, the men's dreams seemed tawdry and dull. *Why?* each man wondered. Then looked at his friends and thought, *Because the team will be splitting up.*

And it was the team that mattered.

There were no obstacles. They weren't following any real roads. They knew to assume the Laotian troops were right behind them, though they had no reason to believe they were. It would not have been the first time an army in Asia had been overconfident in the faith of its air power. The Laotians just might be lazy about it all, and it would take a little time before they discovered that the cache of gold and jewels was missing. Billy Leaps and Applebaum had closed the trapdoor and replaced the chest atop it.

But the team wasn't going to count on Laotian incompetence. They knew better than to assume the easy way out. They had survived in Nam by always giving their enemy all the credit they could. It was dead men who thought the Vietnamese worthless in the battlefield. Survivors had never let an enemy surprise them. That's what made them survivors.

Rosie stopped short. Beeker started to wave him forward but then saw the expression on the black man's face. "They're ahead."

The others froze. As a group they tacked their hearing the way a sailor tacks a sail. They heard the random, secretive noises of small animals, and then, off in the distance, the unmistakable sound made by a group of men moving through the thick undergrowth.

The Black Berets exchanged looks. There was no fear among them. No anticipation. Simply the recognition that the job wasn't over. They had some more killing to do. Beeker—though he hated to admit it—was glad Applebaum was there at this moment. "Applebaum, you take any souvenirs back there in the basement?"

The runt's grin almost split his head. "Well, I did have some space in my pack, so I brought along a few Claymores. Stuck a couple in Harry's pack too. He's so damn strong he never notices a little extra weight."

"Let's use 'em."

"Ambush time?" said Rosie.

"Rock and roll time," said the little blond man.

Beeker moved the team back a hundred yards to a narrow uphill passage.

"Applebaum, set your toys up." The little blond man puffed up, seeming to grow inches in stature. The team leader had given him field command. He was responsible for setting the ambush. He took two of the Claymores and went down the trail thirty meters or so from the team. Placing a mine on each side of the trail, back in the bush ten feet or so, he angled the two mines so their fire would intersect right at the center of the trail. He ran the detonation cords back to where Beeker was setting the team.

"Harry," Billy whispered, "set up some fléchette rounds for that grenade launcher of yours. Cowboy, don't worry about firing. I want you feeding Applebaum's M60. Set it up while he gets the other two Claymores ready. Rosie, you and I are going to take the ends."

Applebaum set the last two Claymores up right in front of the team, again camouflaged and crossing. The killing ground was ready. If the enemy troops entered this block too tightly bunched, the deadly spray of steel balls could kill fifteen or twenty men. If they didn't kill that many, they would stun the rest to the point that the team's attack would be that much more effective. Applebaum slid into concealment with the rest of the team.

"When they start up the hill, get your heads down. We're closer than we should be, but this is all we've got to work with."

Rosie rolled over to look at the little explosives expert. "Are you telling me that you're finally going to blow me away, you little asshole?"

Harry pointed down the trail to indicate that they had company, and all five lay silently, waiting for Applebaum's opening number.

Sweat beaded on Billy Leaps's forehead. He caught sight of the approaching line of troops. They were well uniformed—he could make out the consistency, if not the details, of their dress. They must be government troops, an infantry backup for the choppers that had attacked them at the compound. These weren't irregulars. Beeker had been concerned that they might be a detachment of Kha returning to the house. Not these guys.

He waited. The sweat gathered. If he had dared, he would have wiped it off his brow. But he didn't. He wouldn't chance that the call for attack might come at a moment he was unprepared. He let the salty fluid run down his face. He tilted his head slightly so that the perspiration didn't spill into his eyes. Jesus, Applebaum, come on. They get much closer and we're going to blow us up too.

The blasts were as much a surprise to Beeker as they were to the Laotians.

The blasts illuminated the shocked faces of the government forces. For a split second they were frozen in horror. But then the faces weren't there anymore, and the brilliant white light was tinged with red. Severed legs and arms flew into the air. Bellies opened up, and organs were spilled out, like those of a still-gasping fish, gutted on the cracked boards of an ocean pier. The stench of death soon welled up over the odor of the plastique.

Howls poured through the jungle night. The language of a dying man is universal. The inarticulate cries are the same in Laotian as in English. Each man of the Black Berets thought, *I remember that.*

Not one of the men—not even Applebaum—trusted the explosives to do the job totally. The Claymores hadn't killed all the Laotians. There were still a few of them with rifles, and arms to hold them, and fingers to pull the triggers, and eyes with which to take aim. But the Laotians were frantic, desperate men, and they shot wildly at an unseeable enemy. They knew death stalked them, and they hoped blindly that a dozen bullets randomly fired would preserve them to reach their homes and families.

But the Black Berets' bullets weren't random. Each man had sighted his quarry in the brief flashes of light from the Claymores. The position of each Laotian had been registered. They had raised their M16s and begun a fire that had all the accuracy their enemies lacked. Applebaum ran the M60 full tilt. Beeker hoped he didn't melt the barrel down.

The screams now came staggered. They came one by one. A *plunk* of hot metal burrowing through flesh, a loud groan, a scrabbling against the earth, and then the silence that is greater than any other. The silence that a dead man makes.

The last scrabbling died out, simultaneously with a groan that was full of blood.

The Black Berets waited.

Beeker checked his watch. Either a minute and a half, or two minutes and a half—he couldn't tell which. But that was all it had taken.

"How many were there?" Harry whispered.

Beeker held up his hand sharply—it was still too soon to speak.

They waited a little while longer. Beeker, whose hearing was acute, detected nothing. When he spoke, he spoke in a normal voice.

"About a dozen," he said. "But we're not gonna hang around for a goddamn body count."

"We'll just say fifty-three," said Applebaum, laughing. He was just remembering the inflated figures of the Vietnam war.

"Let's move," said Beeker, turning away. The Black Berets melted into the jungle night again without looking on the faces of the men they had killed.

It was well after dark when they reached the Mekong River. They did not know whether they were upstream or downstream from the place where they had left their boat. They walked upstream on the flip of a Krugerrand that had been part of the cache. When they came to a village, Cowboy bribed a Chinaman who was running a sampan ferry to take them over to Thailand.

The Mekong River on this border between Laos and Thailand was wide and powerful, but slow. Beeker and his men lay low in the sampan and allowed themselves to enjoy the leisurely journey across. You saw the same stars in Indochina that you saw in Louisiana. They kept the rifles ready at their sides, but they felt safer than before.

Applebaum and Harry were joking together, reliving the fight with the Kha, the fight with the Prometheus agents, the helicopter attack. Applebaum told all about blowing open the treasure closet. He continued as they marched through the Thai jungle toward a village marked on their map, where they had hope of hiring a truck that would take them back to Ubon Ratchathani.

Applebaum just didn't stop. When he'd finished all his

stories of the battle in the stone mansion, he began on the forced march through the jungle, and when he was done with that, he made them all remember what training had been like.

No one tried to shut him up. They'd listened before; they'd listen again. Everything they fought . . .

But this was their only mission, the single, false reason for which they'd been brought together again.

"It comes down to Parkes," said Billy Leaps in a quiet voice to Cowboy, and Cowboy just nodded.

Parkes. The man who had done what Billy Leaps now understood was the most dishonorable thing in his—Beeker's—ethic. He had misused the team. The team that had been the best in Vietnam, that had overcome interservice rivalry, constant danger, and omnipresent incompetence all around it. They had done more than survive. In their own way, they had won the war. They had truly won their part of the war in Vietnam. It was the ones around them, the generals and the intelligence officers and the fucked-up strategists in Washington who had lost it.

The United States had lost a war that the real troops—the teams like his—had won.

Beeker remembered the hardest and most difficult lesson that the war had taught. He recalled, as they trod through this Thai jungle, that certain officers had distinguished themselves by nothing but the mistakes they had made. They had made all the mistakes in the book. They had led their troops into obvious ambush, after disdaining to listen to their battle-seasoned noncoms. They had called in air strikes, but because they didn't know how to read maps properly, the coordinates they gave would be off. The bomber crews dropped their deadly cargo on their own troops.

When you've seen a whole team of Americans burning up with napalm that was delivered by the voice order of an officer who had made a "mistake," you have only one option. And you took it, without hesitation, for the sake of men who might die in the future.

The American media had been horrified. That was all right. It was what had to be done. You couldn't stand by and let some asshole whose military training was a semester of ROTC kill your buddies. You let him get ahead of you, and under cover of enemy fire, you shot the most dangerous enemy you knew.

Parkes was that kind of officer. The man who was dangerously incompetent and malicious on top of that. Beeker knew what sort of danger now surrounded him and his men. Beeker's team had killed not only the Kha, but Parkes's Prometheus men. It wouldn't take long before Parkes found out that his poppy fortune was gone and that it had disappeared before the Laotians arrived at the scene. He'd find Beeker, and Beeker's men, and then he'd try to get the money back.

Beeker explained this to Cowboy, to the Greek, to Rosie, and to Applebaum. They talked it over in the truck they had purchased in the Thai village and were driving back to Ubon Ratchathani.

"He'll be after us," Beeker concluded. "If he's not already after us now."

"Let him come," said the Greek.

"I've got this great idea," Applebaum piped up.

Nobody asked what it was. They knew they'd find out.

"Let's stay together," said Applebaum. "For a while. If Parkes is going to come after us, then he'll have a harder time getting to us if we stay together."

For a few moments no one spoke. Give Applebaum credit; sometimes he said the right thing. Each man knew, in his heart, that that was what he wanted. To stay together. To keep the team alive.

"We may not wait," said Billy Leaps.

"What do you mean?" said Cowboy.

"We may not wait for Parkes to come after us," the Cherokee explained. "He betrayed us. He betrayed our team. It may just be time for us to go after him."

A savage attack sets the team up for

COLD VENGEANCE

in Black Berets #2

The boy had been left alone.

The men who called themselves the Black Berets had flown off three weeks ago. The boy was asked to stay and watch the farm, to care for it until they returned. He didn't mind living by himself on the sixty-acre farm a dozen miles outside of Shreveport. That sort of loneliness had been a given in his life. His only break from it had come three months earlier, when he had met Billy Leaps Beeker. Billy Leaps was a Cherokee, just like the boy.

For a short while it had been just the boy and Beeker alone on the farm, and the boy had allowed himself dreams during that time. Billy Leaps brought portions of broth and medicines from the modern doctor and then for hours on end recounted the legends of the Cherokee and the honor of the tribe's warriors. For that—above all—was what the boy had seen in Billy Leaps, that he was a true warrior, just as those in the legends. To hear this man speak of those Cherokee heroes filled the boy with pride. And the hope that he might someday prove himself as well.

Now came the loneliness and the fear that the team that

called itself the Black Berets, with the Cherokee as its leader, would not return from its mission.

The boy thought of that team often. He had wondered, at first, how five men so diverse could work as a unit. And at first they hadn't. But then, gradually, over the period of their three-month training here on the farm, they had come together as a unit. The same unit that had worked in Vietnam a decade earlier.

The men had gathered here on the farm just as the ancient Cherokee warriors had gathered years ago, to train and prepare for war. And they had given the boy hope. Hope that he might have this place as a home, where he could learn to be a warrior himself, a warrior as they were.

The boy thought of all these things as he walked along a disused logging road that wound through the forested portion of Billy Leaps's property. He carried the hunting bow he had found in Beeker's house. He had been desperate to learn the majestic secrets of the rifles the men had practiced with, but they had been preparing for war then and had no time to teach the boy.

In the three weeks of the Black Berets' absence, he had trained himself with it. He strove not only for accuracy, but for ease. He remembered how the team's M16s had seemed to be extensions of their bodies. He wanted to work until the bow felt that way. He succeeded at it, not all the time yet, but on occasion. If only the boy proved himself with the bow and arrow, then perhaps Billy Leaps would be convinced that he, too, could be a warrior.

The boy had made a target range for himself not far from the house. He reached that place now. In his quiver were a dozen arrows. The target, a hundred feet from where he now stood, was merely the upright trunk of a dead tree. He had wrapped it in three cloth rags, one marking the target's head—the height of his own—a second rag the target's heart, and the third its groin. He took an arrow from the quiver and took aim at his target's head. His arm struggled with the great tension of the bow. It always did the first time. Then he could gauge it for the rest of the session. He sighted carefully and released the arrow. It hit right on the mark, just where the head of a man the boy's size would be. The boy smiled.

Then his body froze. So suddenly and completely that even the smile remained graven on his face.

He had heard a strange noise. The boy, who could make no noise himself, was acutely aware of sound. A vehicle was approaching the house. The Black Berets had returned! He turned, and made two hurrying steps toward the logging track that would take him back. Then he stopped, just as suddenly as before. Why had they not returned in the plane, as they had left? He was puzzled, and then nervous. And then cautious.

His caution was confirmed a moment later. The Labrador, tethered by a chair to a corner of the house, began to bark. He would not have had it been Billy Leaps and his men who were returning.

The boy retrieved his arrow from the target and replaced it in his quiver. He crossed stealthily through the forest, approaching the clearing in which Billy Leaps's cabin sat. He was hidden behind underbrush, and he waited as the vehicle approached.

It was a Jeep Wagoneer, a common vehicle in this part of the country. The Wagoneer drove up to the cabin fearlessly, as though the driver knew that the Black Berets were absent. As though he had no idea that anyone had been left to guard the place.

The boy watched. Three men got out of the Wagoneer. He recognized none of them. They were laughing and talking. One man's voice was louder than the others'. The boy heard him say, "Tell y'all something, Parkes is gone, be grateful for this one. Even if there's not gonna be much to it. I don't know nothin' about it, but I'll bet my ass Beeker really fucked 'im over."

All three men moved to the back of the four-wheel drive station wagon. The man who had spoken was obviously in charge. He opened the back and pulled aside a loose tarp. The other two men reached inside and withdrew metal cans, evidently filled with liquid. One went toward the house, the other toward the barn.

The boy knew that the containers held either gasoline or kerosene. They were going to burn the place down.

One man kicked open the door of the cabin and began sloshing the liquid out of the can even before he was well inside. The other man went inside the barn and disappeared from the boy's sight.

The boy was terrified. Not for his personal safety, but because he had been left to watch the farm. He knew what he had to do.

The boy thought for a brief moment.

None of the three had been holding a weapon, though he could see several hunting rifles lying next to the gasoline cans in the rear of the Jeep. He couldn't let the men get to those. And that meant he had to get the man closest to the rifles first. That was the leader. And that was just fine.

The boy moved into the clearing. He avoided the fallen branches he could see and tried not to make any noise whatsoever. He had an arrow out of the quiver, the one he had retrieved from the target.

This first shot had to be perfect. If he missed, they'd be after him with the rifles. And these men were destroyers—they would have no mercy. He had to kill the leader, and not only kill him, but silence him immediately. And he had to hurry.

The boy pulled back the bowstring, aimed the arrow, and as he released it, he prayed a prayer to the gods of the Cherokee.

The razor-sharp point pierced the leader's neck. The arrow sank deep and clean into his throat. His hands jumped up to grab the arrow, though he had no idea what the sudden, painful, unexpected intrusion was. His mouth opened to scream, but what came out was not sound but a geyser of blood that splashed over the side windows of the Jeep, coating them thickly in red.

The blood pulsed out of the hole made in his throat, three times, for three beats of his heart. But then he was dead and his heart wasn't beating anymore, and the fountain of red blood became no more than a sullen, slow stream. He crumpled to the ground, sliding down the side of the car until he came to rest in an awkward crouch beside the back wheel.

The boy was frightened the other two men would hear the noise, or see the blood on the windows, but the men were busy lighting matches. The fire in the house began with a *whoosh*, but before even that sound had peaked into a bellow, it was matched by another from the other side of the clearing. The barn was starting to go up as well.

The boy, with grim determination on his face, ran behind the Jeep. The man who had torched the barn was closer. He would die next. His back was to the boy, his hands on his hips as he stared through the open doors into the brightening interior of the barn. He craned his neck with pleasure to look at the black smoke that had started to seep through the cracks in the roof.

A new arrow was nocked in the boy's bow. The arrow was released with a *twang* that sounded musically in the boy's ear. The aluminum shaft, following the razor-sharp point, sank deep into the man's back. He collapsed onto the earth, within the wavering shadow cast by the burning barn.

Quickly grabbing another arrow from the quiver, the boy raced to the front of the Jeep. One intruder remained. The house that Billy Leaps Beeker had built with his own hands was on fire. The boy could see flames through the open doorway and the window to his left.

The man who had set the fire stood with his back to the house. With an expression of confusion and horror on his face, he was pointing at the body of the group's leader, crouched in the dirt next to the bloodied Jeep. The corpse knelt in a coagulating pool of its own blood.

"Bob!" he screamed. "Bob!"

He started to run for the barn, but after a couple of lurching steps he stopped. He had seen Bob's body lying in the shadows. He went no closer. He looked all round, his head swiveling rapidly.

The boy rose up slowly from behind the station wagon.

The boy's appearance triggered something in the third man. He had seen his two friends dead, and now here was a boy. And the boy was going to pay. The man took two aggressive steps toward the boy. "You little bas—"

He never finished the word or the thought, because there was an arrow in his brain. Four sharpened blades in the shape of an *X* had sliced through his forehead, his skull, and then through the convolutions of his brain, severing all thought, all sensation, all life, in a hundredth of a second. He was, and then, a hundredth of a second later, he ceased to be.

With a fourth arrow strung in readiness the boy went to each of the men to make sure he was dead.

The man he had killed last was certainly dead. The arrow had pierced his brow at a spot directly between his eyes.

He knelt by the back door of the station wagon and peered into the unseeing eyes of the leader of the three men. The wound in his neck was large and gaping, but the blood had ceased to flow. There was proof of death.

The boy moved into the shadow of the barn. The man lying in the dirt there was still alive. The arrow had pierced his back and come out through the front. He had fallen on it, and bent the savage head against the earth. But it had evidently missed his heart, though his labored breathing told that very probably a lung had been punctured.

The boy, who had been squatting off a little ways, stood up. There was only one thing to be done. He took the hunting knife out of his belt, where he always carried it, and walked up to the prone body on the ground. He grabbed the man's head by the hair and lifted it up. He gurgled in his throat, and blood spat up out of his mouth onto the ground. The boy brought the edge of his knife to the front of the man's neck and sliced once across, very hard and quickly.

Blood spewed out in a fan shape.

Cowboy's hangar was the only building left standing, so in the barnlike hangar the boy made himself a bed of straw, and, placing his bow and his arrows beside it, he covered his shivering limbs with a blanket and once more took up his waiting for the return of the Black Berets.